THE PERFECT MATCH
AND OTHER SMALL BITES STORIES

INDIES UNITED PUBLISHING HOUSE, LLC
P.O. BOX 3071
QUINCY, IL 62305-3071

www.indiesunited.net

Dedicated to every person who ever took a chance on an unknown author.
Thank you.

Table of Contents

The Perfect Match..1
   Robert Plant
   Science Fiction
Perennial Guardians...33
   Scott Meehan
   Science Fiction l Historical Fiction
Albert...55
   Donald Firesmith
   Science Fiction | Paranormal
The Adventure...63
   Michael Nelson
   YA Narrative fiction
The First Three Springsteen Albums.....................................84
   D. Krauss
   Coming of Age
From Darkness into Light..109
   Ed DeJesus
   Historical Fiction | Based on True Events
The Outside Clan...123
   Lisa Towles
   Historical Fiction
Blood at the Window...144
   Timothy Baldwin
   Psychological Thriller
There Was an Old Woman Who Thought She Was Dead..............163
   Donna Doty
   Magical Realism

About the Authors..*173*
A little about Indies United...*178*

THE PERFECT MATCH

AND OTHER
SMALL BITES STORIES

AN
INDIES UNITED PUBLISHING HOUSE
MULTI-AUTHOR ANTHOLOGY

INDIES UNITED PUBLISHING HOUSE, LLC

Indies United Publishing House
Small Bites
Grand Prize
Winner
2025
Indies United Publishing House

The Perfect Match

Robert Plant

Science Fiction

Alex was being followed. In fact, everywhere he went and everything he did was tracked down to the minute detail. The coffee he purchased in the morning sent data to several companies that utilize the information to push advertisements and help market their products. The same purchase that fueled his day also fueled these companies with large amounts of data at their disposal. That was how it worked, but it really only scratched the surface.

Now, they had access to his microphone. They could hear his conversations—who he talked to and about what topics. Nothing was off limits. His device worked for him, but it also worked against him by taking away his privacy. They even knew how many times a day he went to the bathroom. They knew what books he read, the movies he watched every Sunday night, and of course, the porn he watched on his phone before bed. Alex believed incognito mode protected him there, but these companies had ways around that.

They also knew Alex had moved to a new city in a new state. He needed a change of pace after striking out with countless women and feeling down on his luck. He thought this change would open up new doors for him. He moved to a college town where there were a ton of possibilities to meet women. Alex hadn't gone to college and worked in retail sales. It wasn't that he wasn't smart enough; he didn't have the drive. He wasn't motivated by money or social status. All he wanted was to meet a nice girl, date her for a while to ensure she was the right fit, ask her to marry him, and then have a dozen kids. In the end, all he wanted was the girl. Someone to love him and hold him like his mother used to when he was a child.

He sat at the bar with his right leg shaking in a nervous twitch, sipping on his Jack and Coke. The flow of customers was steady considering it was a Friday night in a college town. There were patrons all around him, laughing and having a great time, but he sat alone waiting for his friend to join him. He pulled out his phone out of boredom with no one to talk to. He opened his dating app, Konnection, to check his messages, but the little red bubble popped up with only one message. It was from the admin of the app encouraging him to update some information on his profile. He laid the phone on the bar, but before he did, his new device took note of a few things.

First, it knew his location and even marked what stool he sat on at the bar. It used the microphone to record his drink order, and the front camera took note of the shirt he wore and how he styled his hair for the evening.

A young lady with honey hair that curled down past her shoulders walked into the bar in a hurry. She looked rushed, like she wanted to get a drink in before heading home to study for an exam. Alex blushed as she took the seat next to him while she fumbled through her oversized purse for her wallet. Unfortunately, as soon as she looked up to see him staring back at her, she moved over a few seats to keep her distance from him. She was way out of his league, and he drowned himself in his whiskey once he realized he didn't have a shot.

Maybe it was the little bit of acne he had growing on his right cheek. Maybe she could sense he didn't have any confidence in himself—most women could smell that on a man. Or maybe his wide-framed glasses and hunched posture turned her off. He had no way of knowing, and he wasn't about to ask her.

"Dude!" Alex's friend Noah screamed from across the bar. He walked through the crowd and slapped Alex on the shoulder. "What's goin' on, my man?"

"Not much."

Noah loosened the scarf around his neck and wiped the snow off his shoulders. He brushed his hands through his dark hair in James Dean fashion. He had the looks of James Dean, and his confidence came off like Sinatra, especially with his dark hair pulled back. Regardless, the ladies loved it, and they loved him. The way he conducted himself and the air of confidence he brought into a room every time he walked through the door.

"Did I just see you strike out? *Again?*" Noah motioned to the bartender. "I'll have a rum and Coke."

"No, you jackass. I didn't even say anything to her."

"Well, I saw her change seats and look at you like you're the Grim Reaper. We gotta get you laid tonight."

Alex sipped his drink without saying anything, either out of embarrassment or frustration. Maybe both.

"I mean, look at all these beautiful women around here." Noah waved his arms around, gesturing to several different groups of women, some of whom took notice. There was that air of confidence fogging up the room. "Aren't you glad you finally decided to move out here with your best bud?"

Alex nodded his head in agreement and sipped his drink.

The woman who had moved a few seats down gazed over at Noah and smiled. She sipped her rose-colored wine and turned toward the door, putting her back toward him.

"Watch this," Noah whispered into Alex's ear as he stood up from his stool.

Alex could hear mumbles of them talking under the tone of the crowd in the bar, but he couldn't make out exactly what they were saying. Within a minute, Noah had his arm around her, and they were laughing while they clinked their drinks together. It was like they had been friends for years. Alex couldn't understand how Noah could turn a complete stranger into someone who adored him after barely even knowing them. He did it all the time, and it drove Alex crazy.

He decided to ignore them and watch the baseball game on the television directly in front of him. The batter on the screen struck out, and Alex knew how he felt.

Noah came back after a few minutes and put his arm around Alex. "Alright, man. This is your chance. My new friend Mary over there has a friend for you. Don't fuck this up."

Alex glanced over and saw a somewhat pretty woman with natural features sitting next to the girl who had dissed him earlier and was now giving Noah "fuck me" eyes. This new girl looked like someone on his level, and he thought he might actually have a chance.

They all hung out, taking shots and telling stories, which mostly came from Noah. He could hold the attention of a room no matter the circumstances, and both girls seemed to eat it up. Alex's awkwardness got the best of him, and he had a hard time connecting with Mary's friend Amber.

Every movie Alex brought up, she hated. He loved meat; she was a vegan. He liked to play the popular, yet very nerdy, board game Dragons and Dwarves, but she hadn't even heard of the game. While Noah and Mary had their hands all over each other giggling every other second, Alex and Amber looked like two sore thumbs sitting across from each other.

By the end of the night, Noah went home with Mary, and Alex went home alone. Amber was very sweet and let him down easy, but it still burned at him that he couldn't make a connection with her.

Alex opened his phone in bed later that night, hoping to see a message in his Konnection app, but it read, "No New Messages." He closed his phone and looked up at the ceiling, feeling the room spin from the alcohol. His eyes fluttered closed as he went off to dream about his future life with a beautiful wife and kids running around their house. Despite being alone that night, he slept with a smile—although, he wasn't *really* alone. His phone was always with him. Always watching.

His phone buzzed on his nightstand early the next morning like it was telling Alex he needed to wake up and start playing with it. It was like a little kid waking up his parents to play, but really, it was Noah asking him to meet him at the diner for breakfast. Still, his phone had plenty to track that morning—how long he slept, the news articles he read while brushing his teeth, what clothes he put on for the day, what music he listened to while he walked to the diner, and what route he walked.

It wasn't only his phone doing the tracking. Security cameras on the street observed who he made eye contact with, what stores drew his attention, and what ads he took note of during his walk. Almost everything about this young man's life was tracked by the technology around him, right down to his watch recording each and every heartbeat he had.

Alex located his friend sitting in a booth at the back of the diner. The waitress refilled Noah's coffee, and Alex asked for one as well.

"Sup?" Noah's voice was low and worn out.

"Late night?"

"You could say that. I haven't slept."

"Must've been a good night with that girl you met then."

"Correction. *Girls.*"

"No way! How?"

Noah wore sunglasses to help wane his hangover, and he tipped them down to look Alex right in the eyes. "You. All thanks to you."

"Pff. What?!"

"Yeah, that other girl ended up being her roommate. You struck out with her pretty hard, and she was jealous of her friend. I was able to spread the love though. If you know what I mean." As he said it, Noah spread jam across his toast. "Sorry for already ordering. I'm starving."

"I bet." Jealousy overtook Alex and he looked away depressingly. *Why is Noah so lucky with girls? Why was he born with his good looks?* Envy crept into his thoughts.

"Look." Noah cut into his stack of pancakes as he talked. "You're not gonna meet girls at bars, Alex. You read books. You watch old episodes of *The Twilight Zone* and *Star Trek*. Girls who are into that kinda stuff aren't going to be available for pickup at a bar. Those girls want a bad boy who drives a muscle car or a motorcycle."

"You think you're a bad boy? You don't drive a muscle car or have a motorcycle."

"Yeah, but I have good looks so I can get away with it."

Alex rolled his eyes at that one. "Alright, hot shot. Where am I going to meet girls that are more my speed then?"

Right as he finished his sentence, Alex's phone flashed an alert onto his lock screen—it was an email from a new dating app. Perfect Match promised Alex they'd found his soulmate. There were dozens of girls who were already interested in dating him, according to the email.

"What the hell?" Alex mumbled under his breath. He wondered how these girls knew who he was or anything about him.

"What? What is it?" Noah shoved a huge pile of pancakes into his mouth.

Alex ignored him and kept reading the email. Profile pictures and notes from different girls made up the rest of the email, and Alex's skepticism melted away. For example, one of the messages said she also loved Star Trek and The Twilight Zone. Alex thought it was a strange coincidence they were talking about those shows only a moment ago.

"If you don't tell me what the hell you're looking at, I'm gonna throw the rest of my pancakes at you."

"Have you heard of this new dating app, Perfect Match?"

"Nope." Noah became agitated at Alex for answering his question with another question.

"Well, this email is saying there are dozens of girls who are interested in me. I have no idea how they found out anything about me, though. This girl wrote to me saying she likes *The Twilight Zone* and *Star Trek*. We were just talking about that. Isn't that crazy?"

"Sounds like you struck gold, my man! You gotta write her back. Is she hot?"

"She's attractive for sure." Alex turned his phone to show Noah her picture. "Looks like she's way out of my league."

In fact, all the girls featured in the email looked out of his league. Most of them with wavy, blonde hair running past their shoulders and sparkling eyes gleaming at the camera. Not only were they all attractive, but they also had the same interests as Alex. Especially one girl, Jessica. She looked stunning, and her blue eyes locked on Alex's like a painting that follows you with its eyes when you walk by it in a haunted house.

"You should write her back. That Konnection app sucks, and you haven't had much success at the bars."

"I dunno, man. This seems…weird. Like it's too good to be true."

"If I were you, I'd give it a shot. You gotta keep putting yourself out there, or you're gonna end up an old lump of clay sitting in your recliner watching *Star Trek* reruns."

Alex thought about how everything always fell into Noah's lap. He always got what he wanted. Maybe this time the universe was turning things around in his favor. Maybe it was his turn to have something fall into his lap.

What were the chances the first girl he met on this app would end up being the one? It had only been a few weeks, and they were texting each other constantly. She knew *everything* about *Star Trek*. She even knew about the unaired pilot where Captain Pike was actually at the helm of the Enterprise. What beautiful 24-year-old girl knew about that? He was infatuated with her. Every free second he had in his day was dedicated to texting Jessica.

Alex: *where have you been all my life?*
Jessica: *right here. waiting for you.*
Alex: *it's hard to believe you don't have a boyfriend. what am i missing?*
Jessica: *i have very specific taste Alex. i'm not looking for some fling either. i want to find someone real. i want to live long and prosper with someone :)*
Alex: *you could have any guy you want. why me? what makes me so special?*
Jessica: *you're adorable. plus i'm not completely sold on you…yet.*
Alex: *maybe i can change that. let's meet in person. coffee tomorrow morning?*
Jessica: *coffee…that's boring. how about dinner? i know a really good place.*

Jumping straight to dinner seemed aggressive to Alex, even though they'd already been talking for a few weeks. He had seen this play by girls on these apps in the past and had been burned. He would take them out to this fancy dinner, they'd stumble through awkward conversations, he'd pay the bill, and he'd never hear from them again. Ghosted.

Despite his reservations about joining the app and now dinner, he felt drawn to Jessica. He had this feeling in the pit of his stomach that made him anxious but in a good way. Something he'd never felt before. Maybe it was the beginning of something special, and it scared him a little bit.

All he knew was he was sick of being alone, and it was time to make a change.

Alex stood outside the restaurant, waiting for Jessica to arrive, with his hands fidgeting inside his pockets. He had never been this nervous for a date in his life. Looking at the place from the outside even intimidated him. He didn't even think he could afford to eat at a place like this.

Jessica pulled up in her car—a smooth-looking Lexus —while Alex had walked because he didn't even have a car. There wasn't a need for one in the city really, but still, he felt diminished knowing she drove a car probably worth more than he made in a year. He wondered how a young girl in her twenties could even afford a car like that. Maybe her parents were rich.

Jessica popped out of the driver seat, closed the door, and smiled from ear to ear as she walked up to Alex.

"Wow!" Alex's jaw almost dropped to the ground.

"Are you referring to my dress or the car?" Jessica twirled in a circle creating a flow on the skirt of her dress that would hypnotize almost any man.

"Would you be upset if I said both?"

"Ha! You're so adorable." Jessica leaned in and gave him a kiss on his cheek. She stayed close to his face, peering into his eyes, trying to hypnotize him in case the skirt didn't do the trick.

Alex's face flushed, and he awkwardly glanced over to the door of the restaurant. "I probably shouldn't say this…but I dunno if I can afford this place."

"Who said you were buying? C'mon." She grabbed his hand and pulled him to the door where he graciously opened it for her. She curtsied at him. "Aw, thank you. Such a gentleman."

They walked up to the concierge, and Jessica gave the hostess her name for the reservation.

"Is it just me or wouldn't it be so cool if all doors made the same sound from *Star Trek*?" Jessica mimicked the futuristic swoosh of a door opening and closing like the show. It almost sounded perfect to Alex like she had a recording of the sound playing from her mouth.

"I was just saying that to my friend the other day!"

"No way!" She gently slapped him on the shoulder and proceeded to cuddle into it while they waited for their table to be ready. It was like this was their hundredth date, not their first. They had an instant connection, and it seemed like Jessica didn't want to let go of Alex. It was a dream for him to have this beautiful girl all over him. His tensions loosened, and he soaked in everything about her. How her hair glistened in the light with every turn of her head. The way she smiled out of the corner of her mouth. Those blue eyes pierced his soul every time she looked at him.

While Jessica leaned against his shoulder, Alex reached down and pinched his arm.

"What was that?" She pulled back confused.

"I had to pinch myself to make sure I wasn't dreaming."

Jessica immediately grabbed him by the back of the head and kissed him on the lips. It was a gentle kiss with only a little bit of tongue. It surprised Alex, but once his brain comprehended what was happening, he sunk into her and kissed her back. Usually, this happened at the end of a date. Well, not for Alex, but that was what he saw in the movies.

They were seated in the back of the restaurant with dimmed lighting and a view of the ocean behind the restaurant. It was the best seat in the house. Alex picked up the menu and noticed the prices.

"Okay…I really can't afford this."

"I told you this is on me. You're a chivalrous guy, Alex, but I also know you're not egotistical enough to let this bother you. Besides, who's to say which gender should purchase the meal on a first date."

"In that case, I'll have the steak and lobster."

Jessica boomed out a raucous laugh. "You are so funny I can't stand it. Just make sure you leave room for dessert." She winked at him, making it seem like she wasn't talking about food.

Most men would insist on paying, but she knew Alex was easily persuaded. In fact, that was one of the main traits she had honed in on when reviewing his profile. She knew she could manipulate him and get him to do whatever she pleased. Jessica wasn't hungry and decided to push things forward a little more quickly than anticipated. Usually, she'd at least allow the courtesy of one last meal for her candidates but not tonight. She was under orders to get the job done as quickly as possible.

They both continued to look at the menu, but Jessica's eyes sharply peered over her menu at Alex. She placed her menu down on the table as the waiter approached.

"Good evening." The waiter stood at their table with his hands behind his back. "Welcome to the…"

"I'm sorry, but may we please have another minute."

The waiter nodded and walked off.

Jessica leaned across the table displaying her well-rounded breasts to Alex as she tucked her hair behind her ear. "Let's get outta here."

"What? Really? I thought this was going well, no?" Alex immediately thought he had blown the date already.

"It is…I just thought we could maybe have more fun

back at my place. I have a frozen pizza, and we can watch *Terminator.*"

"Which one?"

"Two of course. That's the best one. Everyone knows that."

"It's one of the few times. . . " Then in unison. ". . . the sequel was better than the original."

Jessica knew Alex would say that because he had posted about it being one of his favorite movies and used that exact line in his post. She knew almost everything about him, including ways to get to his heart, like suggesting frozen pizza and T2.

They stood and quickly walked out of the restaurant like they were ditching class in high school. They bonded in that moment of defiance together. Even though they weren't breaking any rules, it still felt like they were.

Jessica managed to keep her hands on Alex the entire car ride back to her place. She held his hand for a bit before running her hand down his thigh toward his groin. Alex had never been with a woman so aggressive, and he loved every second of it. He couldn't keep his eyes off her and barely watched the road. If you asked him how they got to her house, he wouldn't have a clue. He stayed fixated on Jessica the entire ride.

It wasn't until they pulled up to a large black gate that Alex finally looked out of the car.

"Woah. This is the entrance to your house?"She pressed a button on the roof of the car to open the gate and smiled at him.

The driveway ran through woods for more than a mile, winding all the way up to a huge house secluded from civilization. It was modern, yet comforting as you approached the house with its sparkling white siding and wood trim. Alex noticed the view of the ocean as they pulled around to the side of the house in front of the garage. The house sat on an elevated lot overlooking the Pacific, which appeared to be about a hundred feet below them. It was a spectacular view, especially with the half-moon making its way to the horizon. It was bright, one side illuminated and the dark side still hiding its face in the shadows. Alex hated heights, and looking over the cliff sent a chill up his spine and made his palms sweat.

Jessica pressed another button, and the garage opened. There were a few other cars in the garage, and it made Alex wonder if there were other people there.

"Do you have company over? Please tell me one of these cars isn't your husband's."

"No, silly! Do you see a ring on this finger?" She held up her left hand.

"Sorry." Alex blushed in embarrassment. "I didn't think you'd have this many cars. What do you do for a living?"

"I work in the healthcare industry. I do research and development. R and D, they call it."

"Are you a doctor?"

She laughed. "No. I just give the doctors what they need to get their job done." Again, she rubbed her hand into his inner thigh as she rolled the car into the garage. Each time she rubbed him, his heart rate jumped, but his nerves seemed to calm all at the same time.

Alex still felt a little uneasy about going into a stranger's house. He hadn't found himself in a situation like this…ever. He had been lucky a few years back and actually got a girl to come back to his place. She wasn't impressed and never called him back. He couldn't help but think why this rich and beautiful woman would want to be with him. Most men who are down on their luck with women question the first one that comes along and actually shows them attention.

Jessica removed her hand from Alex to turn off the car. She gave him a mischievous glance and encouraged him to follow her into the house. "C'mon. Let's go."

She led him into the house and offered him something to drink. He declined alcohol because he wanted to be able to remember everything about this night. He might not get another night like this ever again in his life. Jessica pulled out a water bottle from the fridge, and while he chugged from the bottle, she stepped behind him to help take off his jacket, rubbing her hands up and down his torso. For a moment, it felt like she was scanning him like one of those TSA agents at the airport would with their wand.

Jessica lightly pinched his nipples, started giggling, and ran away from him with encouragement for him to follow. "You said you wanted to see the *Terminator*, right?"

He playfully jogged after her, and they met at the top of the stairs to the basement. He pushed his lips against hers when their bodies collided. He was over the moon. He felt like he'd do anything for this woman. This angel had fallen into his lap.

She smiled at him and started down the stairs. "Come with me if you want to live." Alex dropped his head back, laughing at her reference to the movie. Alex had been falling for Jessica the entire night, but that sent him over the edge.

The theater room in the basement looked like a real theater, with rows of leather chairs and couches, bean bags, a popcorn machine, a bar, and a huge projection screen that took up almost the entire wall.

"Wow! This is amazing."

"You like it? It's my favorite room in the entire house."

"I mean…I don't know what to say." Alex lived for movies. He had dreamed of owning a house with a room like this. He'd never have to go to the movies and sit in front of some fat slob shoving popcorn and candy into their mouth again. Or have to listen to those annoying teenage girls gossiping during the entire movie instead of actually watching it. He could have the privacy he wanted with the authentic movie experience.

Jessica picked a couch and patted the seat to get Alex to sit with her. It was like an owner calling their dog up onto the couch to snuggle in for a movie. She pressed a button on her remote, and the screen came to life.

A video started to play.

"We don't always get second chances in life."

A woman started the advertisement, and it was one of those cliché commercials for medication that have kids running around chasing butterflies and a father and son fishing on a lake.

"With Regenerate, you now have that chance. Every organ, every blood type. We have your match and can give you an opportunity to receive your requested transplant within 24 hours."

Alex looked over at Jessica who was zoned into the TV, not making any movements or even blinking. She must really be into this commercial he thought. She is in the medical field after all.

The woman continued speaking about the various case studies and how they had saved thousands of lives in their company's short history.

"We're changing the world one transplant at a time."

The commercial ended.

The screen remained dark, and a light came on over a door next to the screen. A woman walked out in a business suit with glasses and long blonde hair that had been straightened out flat. She had a serious look on her face as she scanned her clipboard while standing in front of the blank projector screen.

"You must be…Alex. Welcome."

Alex noticed she had the same voice as the woman from the commercial.

"Who are you? What's going on?" He turned to Jessica. "I thought you said no one else was here."

Jessica didn't move an inch and continued her zoned-out stare at the screen.

"Welcome to the Regenerate headquarters. My name's Rebecca. What did you think of our newest commercial?"

Alex hadn't freaked out yet, but he was definitely growing concerned with each second that passed. "You 3-D print organs. Seems like a huge advancement in healthcare technology. Can I go now?"

He stood from his seat looking to make an exit, but Rebecca encouraged him to stay seated. "I just have a few more questions."

"If I answer them, can I go?"

"Of course. However, I'm hoping you'll want to work here once I tell you more."

"Work here?"

"Yes, we're in need of backfilling a position, and you're a perfect candidate for the job."

"Okay. . ." Alex looked over at Jessica, still in the same position. "What the fuck is wrong with her? Why isn't she moving?"

"I'll explain everything. I just need to ask you a few

questions before we can move on to the next step of your orientation. Can you confirm your blood type is A-positive?"

"Yeah, it is. How did you know that?"

"You donated blood to the Red Cross a few years back, and we work with them."

Learning that Regenerate worked with the American Red Cross made Alex feel a little more relaxed, but Jessica's dormant state still worried him.

"Are you a smoker?"

"I've never smoked a day in my life."

"Good. Good." Rebecca marked her clipboard a few times. "Your family history looks pretty normal. Okay, I think we're good to move on."

As soon as she finished speaking, the screen started to roll up, revealing a window. Rebecca motioned for Alex to come up to take a look. He stood and kept his eyes on Jessica, wondering why she had remained dormant this entire time. As he approached the window, he couldn't believe what he saw.

There were rows of humans lined up on metal structures for what looked like a mile long. Each person had a shaved head and tubes sticking in and out of them in several places. Their arms were spread wide, and they would have all looked like Jesus on the cross, except their legs were spread apart to form a human X. Alex scanned the area and noticed all the equipment. The facility must have cost billions of dollars to build and set up. It looked like a scene out of *The Matrix* with all the bodies lined up.

"Every time you see Reggie…"

A drone with robotic arms quickly flew across the window and zoomed away. It hovered over one of the women, and red lasers shot out from the machine like it was scanning a barcode.

"…it means a life is about to be saved. We get dozens of requests a day from all around the world for people needing organs to survive. Our tech is able to scan internal organs without invading the rep, and we 3-D print the organ to send it out to those in need. The perfect match every single time. We save dozens of lives a day, and soon we'll be able to help every single person across the globe in need of an organ to survive."

"But these are real humans you're scanning. Are they alive?"

"Yes, but they're heavily sedated."

"How can you do that? You're holding these people hostage and stealing their organs. This is so fucked up!"

"Alex, calm down. All of them have agreed to this. They know it's for the greater good. Let me ask you this. Would you sacrifice yourself to save hundreds, maybe thousands of other people?"

"I mean…yeah." For the first time, Alex realized that he could end up being one of the reps on this human farm for organs. He also thought about how the black market for organs had really changed from what he'd seen in the movies. "This is crazy. I can't do this. I want to go home. Now!"

"But you just said you want to help."

"No, I didn't. I'm not agreeing to this."

"Yes, you did." Rebecca nodded her head like she was telling someone to do something.

Suddenly, Jessica was standing right behind him, and a recording started to play. Her lips weren't moving, but the sound was definitely coming from her.

"Would you sacrifice yourself to save hundreds, maybe thousands of other people?" The recording of Rebecca played, then Alex's response.

"I mean…yeah."

"I mean…yeah."

"I mean…yeah."

Alex started to feel faint. His vision swirled around, and he lost his balance, falling into one of the leather chairs. It could have been shock, but then he realized something as he reached for the water bottle Jessica gave him. He picked it up and tried to bring it into focus as his vision blurred. The medicine in the bottle worked as a time-release, weakening his muscles to avoid any chance of escape. His body felt heavy, and suddenly he couldn't move at all. This is what paralysis must feel like, he thought.

"You see, Jessica here is programmed to know everything about you. That's why it was so easy for her to connect with you. We used all the public data that you put out onto the internet to develop a report on you and your life. We need to ensure that all of our candidates fit certain criteria in order for them to be able to qualify for harvesting. We recently lost our white male with an A-positive blood type. You were a perfect match, so we dispatched one of our female androids based on your sexual preferences and had her begin communications with you through our 'dating' app. Enter Jessica."

Alex looked over at Jessica standing at attention. Everything about her seemed so real on the outside, yet everything inside so fake. He had been catfished by an android. His eyes took one final swirl, and he lost consciousness.

Beep. Beep. Beep…

The beeping sound woke Alex from his dormant state. One of the tubes connected to his body had come loose, and an alert continuously beeped to warn central command of the issue. This particular tube was responsible for keeping Alex unconscious. The tube hadn't been properly connected, and the pressure eventually pushed the tube out of place. A stream of sleeping gas shot out from the tube into the air, making a hissing sound.

It took a moment for Alex to realize where he was and what was happening. He only had a minute before Reggie would show up to check on the issue. He looked around and saw the other people surrounding him in the vast human farm for organs. He lifted one of his arms and rubbed his eyes. He was surprised his hands and legs weren't restrained, but it was unnecessary considering all the human subjects were being fed sleeping gas to keep them in a comatose state.

Alex rubbed his hands through the stubble of his newly buzzed head. He started to pull out the tubes connected to his body, one by one. Each tube released liquids and gasses to help keep him barely alive for harvest. With every tube pulled, another beeping sound started. By the time he finished removing the tubes, there was a symphony of alerts calling to central command for assistance. At this point, he had only seconds before Reggie would find him.

He tried to stand, but his legs felt like Jello. He started to slap his legs to try to get the blood flowing. He beat at them and eventually started shaking them back and forth while crippled on the ground. He felt the nerves come back into his right leg, and he figured that was all he needed to start his escape. His left leg limped behind him as he trudged along down his row past the other humans. All different races, genders, and blood types carefully mapped out and ready for harvest. Their blank faces somehow stared at him even though their eyes were closed.

Alex slowly got all the feeling back into his body and kept moving forward. That's what he told himself: "Keep moving forward. Just keep moving forward." He finally found an exit that led to a stairwell and began his ascent back to ground level. There was only one way to go anyway, and that was up.

A drone had finally come to Alex's farming location and alerted Rebecca that one of her subjects had escaped. She called on two of her male androids to search the area and find him. Not only did these droids serve as security for Rebecca, but she also used them to catfish women, or anyone with a sexual preference for men, the same way she had used Jessica on Alex. With a small army of droids at her command, she was able to create her organ farm and keep it running with little to no issue. This wasn't the first time a human had attempted an escape, and it wouldn't be the last. She sat in her office chair, staring at the photo of Alex, knowing that he would never leave her farm. A wicked smile formed on her face, but deep inside she knew what she was doing saved thousands of lives.

Alex made it to the top of the stairs and flung open the door. His naked body was hit with the morning sun as he shielded his eyes from the bright light. His breath was visible in the cold air as he panted. The door sat on the side of a shed in the backyard with the house a few hundred yards away. He turned to the woods and ran, his footprints leaving a trail in the snow.

He ran until his feet started to bleed from the branches and rocks scattered along the ground. They started to numb from the cold with each bloody imprint. His life was at stake, and he'd do whatever it took to escape.

Alex hid behind a tree and debated trying to climb up. His breath clouded the air in front of him, making it harder for him to see. His chest heaved in and out as he tried to regain his breath and slow his nerves to make the right decision. Cold, naked, and weak, he knew there was only one thing to do—run.

He could hear someone behind him now, starting to gain on him, and he increased his speed out of pure adrenaline. The two male droids used their optical heat sensors to scan the area and locate Alex. They spotted him and started to run toward him like a cheetah after its prey.

Alex ran as fast as he could and felt them gaining on him. He looked back while he ran and didn't see the end of the tree line coming. Unfortunately for him, the end of the tree line was also the edge of the cliff that dropped into the Pacific. On his way down, he knew it was the end. His body hit the ocean with enough force to push his brain into his skull, instantly killing him.

The two droids made it to the edge of the cliff and looked down at Alex's floating body moving from wave to wave around the rocky shoreline. One of them scanned for any sign of life. It zeroed in on Alex's heart, and blood pumped through this critical organ for the last time. A 3-D copy of his heart would never save a life in need.

The droid finished its scan. "Subject 5732, deceased."

"I've sent the report back to Rebecca. She said leave him."

"Looks like she'll have to find another one."

The two droids turned and walked back to the farm.

He sat at the bar rocking his leg up and down in anticipation. He didn't get nervous, but this felt different. Maybe it was because he never really did the online dating thing. He was good with women in person. He hated texting. He'd rather meet a girl at a bar or a grocery store. He could use his slick syntax to sway almost any girl into his arms. But this wasn't any girl. This was the perfect girl.

He downed the last sip of his drink and motioned to the bartender for another. He needed the liquid courage to calm his nerves. His eyes fixated on the door every five seconds waiting for her to walk through. Finally, she did. Even though he had seen her picture online, it was love at first sight.

She looked the same as before, except for one detail. Her hair was now red. That was his preference. She slowly walked toward him, and he eyed her up with his mouth agape. She was his dream girl, and for once he couldn't speak. Yeah, he had good looks, but his bread and butter was how he could swoon a woman with his words.

Finally, she broke the silence. "You must be Noah."

"And you must be Jessica."

Indies United Publishing House
2nd
Place
Small Bites
Short Story Contest
2025

Perennial Guardians

Scott Meehan

Science Fiction l Historical Fiction

Commander Eliot Henson and his crew are sent back in time to 1863 during the Civil War. Their mission? To make sure that history takes place the way it happened.

In 2030, Space Command Intelligence Officer Major Asha Hawkins, discovers that an alien entity entered the Civil War time period to alter history. By keeping General Stonewall Jackson alive at Chancellorsville, Confederate Army General Robert E. Lee wins a tremendous victory at Gettysburg. The results lead to the Southern States triumph, continued slavery, and a complete secession from what we know as the United States.

This change in history, unless aligned correctly by Henson and his team, will lead to cataclysmic results for the split nation going into the 20th Century...one that the entire country will not survive.

Commander's log, 2030 AD (and/or) April 30, 1863
– Commander's Log
April 30, 1863 / 2030 AD

After navigating the quantum zone—a non-relativistic continuum connecting myriad worlds—we have successfully touched down in the rolling green hills of western Maryland. This landscape, bathed in the golden hues of spring, stands in stark contrast to the metallic confines of our ship, yet it is here, amidst the tranquil pastures, that our critical mission begins.

Utilizing the light-speed breakaway factor, we pierced the fabric of time itself, emerging in the 19th century on a pivotal day in April 1863. Space Command, mere hours ago in 2030 AD, briefed us on a perturbation in the logical framework of history. An anomaly had been detected—an unknown force tampering with the timeline. Our objective: correct this interference and ensure the course of American history remains unaltered, safeguarding the future of our nation and, by extension, the world.

Failure is not an option. The ripple effect of a single altered event could cascade into a catastrophic divergence, plunging humanity into an abyss of chaos and uncertainty. We carry the weight of centuries on our shoulders, but with our combined expertise, I am confident in our ability to succeed.

Accompanying me on this high-stakes journey are three exceptional individuals, each chosen for their unique skills and unwavering resolve. Chief Medical Officer Dr. Dan Kelley, whose medical prowess is rivaled only by his quick thinking under pressure, will ensure our health and resilience. Major Asha Hawkins, my first officer, is a trailblazer and the first female Green Beret. She brings unparalleled tactical acumen and unyielding determination. Lastly, our Technical Science Officer, the android Cyrix—C01Y2R1I0X—possesses an analytical mind and adaptability that transcends human limitations. Her synthetic intuition and rapid processing are invaluable assets in this temporal odyssey.

Together, we form an unbreakable unit, each well-versed in the others' strengths and weaknesses. We are not merely a crew; we are a family bound by a singular mission: to protect the integrity of history and ensure that the future remains bright.

As the sun dips below the horizon, casting long shadows over these verdant hills, we ready ourselves for the challenges ahead. History awaits, and we are its guardians.

—EH

Commander's log, 2030 AD (and/or) May 2, 1863

We spent two days on the ground preparing for the

mission before making our move. Today, we arrived at a remote ridge just outside Chancellorsville, Virginia. The late afternoon sunbathed the landscape in a golden glow, casting long shadows across the rolling hills. This was the setting for one of the most critical moments in American history. On this day, General Stonewall Jackson would execute a daring flanking maneuver, a tactical masterstroke that would lead to the Confederate victory at the Battle of Chancellorsville.

History records that Jackson's bold march of thirty thousand men swung behind General Hooker's army, leading to a devastating attack on the Union's right flank. This triumph, a pinnacle of Confederate military strategy, left President Lincoln reeling in anger and disbelief. Yet, this mission's significance transcended the immediate battle—it was a precursor to Gettysburg.

A Confederate victory there would alter the course of history, dooming the Union and reshaping the world as we know it.

The anxiety of what lay ahead gnawed at me, though I drew confidence from Cy's unwavering composure. Our task was clear: we had to ensure that history unfolded as it should, which meant allowing the tragic yet pivotal shooting of General Jackson. It was a grim necessity to prevent a future of division, slavery, and a fractured America.

The complication? An enemy agent—a Chinese AI shapeshifter—had infiltrated this moment in history. Its mission: prevent Jackson's death, ensuring the South's victory at Gettysburg and the Union's subsequent downfall. If the shapeshifter succeeded, the ramifications would be catastrophic. The United States would never reunite, and the balance of power would shift dramatically, with Mexico emerging as a dominant force in the western hemisphere.

As the sun dipped below the horizon, casting the battlefield into twilight, Major Hawkins, Cy and I moved into position. Equipped with her advanced detection capabilities, Cy identified the shapeshifter—a Confederate soldier poised to intervene at the critical moment. The impostor approached Jackson's men, mimicking a Southern drawl with chilling accuracy.

"Evening boys," the shapeshifter greeted them, exuding an air of familiarity and authority. The men responded with trust, oblivious to the deception.

"Lieutenant Morrison wants you boys to head back to camp," it continued. "Get some rest. I'll take it from here. The Lieutenant anticipates a quiet night."

The soldiers, weary and eager for respite, complied. This was the moment of truth. Asha steadied her breath, her sniper rifle trained on the shapeshifter. One shot was all she needed. Time seemed to slow as she exhaled, her finger tightening on the trigger.

Pop.

The shapeshifter crumpled to the ground, and chaos erupted. "Yanks!" I shouted, adding to the confusion.

The Confederate soldiers, caught off guard, fired wildly into the night, believing they were under attack. Amidst the chaos, Jackson's men appeared, and the scene played out exactly as history dictated.

Lieutenant Morrison's desperate cries to cease fire were met with disbelief. "It's a lie," a rebel shouted back, and the firing continued. Jackson was hit, his fate sealed. History had been preserved.

Cy confirmed the shapeshifter's demise, and we retreated under the cover of darkness, returning to our cloaked cycles. The mission was a success. We had prevented a catastrophic divergence in the timeline, securing the future of the United States.

As we made our way back to the ship, the weight of what we had done settled over me. The cost of preserving history was high, but the stakes had been even higher. We had played our part, ensuring that the sacrifices of the past paved the way for a unified future.

—EH

Commander's log, 2030 AD (and/or) May 5, 1863

Stonewall Jackson succumbed to his wounds three days after being shot by his own men—a turning point that altered the command structure of the Confederate army. His death forced General Lee to reorganize his two large corps into three, a decision with profound implications for the battles to come.

Lt. Gen. James Longstreet took command of the First

Corps, a seasoned and reliable leader. However, the Second Corps was now under Lt. Gen. Richard S. Ewell, and the Third Corps under Lt. Gen. A.P. Hill—both of whom had previously served under Jackson as division commanders. This promotion thrust them into a new level of responsibility, a significant shift that would test their mettle in the critical engagements ahead.

Equally notable was the role of Maj. Gen. J.E.B. Stuart, who commanded the Cavalry Division. His actions—or lack thereof—would play a pivotal part in the next chapter of the war. But that analysis will come in due course.

For now, the mission's success was clear. History was back on course. The precarious balance of the timeline had been restored. Jackson's death, while tragic, ensured that the events leading to the Battle of Gettysburg would unfold as they originally had, keeping the Union's path to victory intact.

Our team had intervened decisively, and the weight of our actions was matched only by the magnitude of their impact. The course of American history had been preserved.

More challenges lay ahead, but for this moment, we could breathe a sigh of relief. The future of the United States was, once again, secure.

—EH

Commander's log, 2030 AD (and/or) May 6, 1863

Turns out, we only thought our mission was complete. History had been restored, Stonewall Jackson had succumbed to his wounds, and the timeline appeared intact. Preparations for our return to 2030 AD were underway, and we allowed ourselves a moment of quiet celebration. However, our brief reprieve was abruptly shattered by an urgent signal from Future Command 2030.

Cy received the transmission, her synthetic voice cutting through our preparations. "Stop packing, we must stay."

We turned to her, stunned, as if she had just malfunctioned. Her expressionless gaze only added to the surreal weight of her words.

"I am serious," she continued. "Command intelligence has uncovered another shapeshifter presence, this one in the vicinity of Gettysburg itself."

A collective groan filled the room, punctuated by a few choice expletives from Dr. Kelley. The reality of our extended mission sank in quickly. The battle of Gettysburg was a pivotal moment in American history, and any disruption could spell disaster for the Union— and for the future we were fighting to protect.

Without hesitation, we set about developing a new plan. The stakes had risen, and the complexity of our task multiplied. This was no longer a single mission; it was a campaign to ensure the continuity of history itself.

Our focus now shifted to Gettysburg. We needed to

identify the new shapeshifter, anticipate its moves, and neutralize the threat before it could alter the course of the battle. Every moment counted, and the weight of the mission pressed heavily on our shoulders.

As we worked through the night, the gravity of our situation became ever clearer. The fight was far from over. Gettysburg awaited.

—EH

Commander's log, 2030 AD (and/or) May 19, 1863

It has been two weeks since our successful mission at Chancellorsville, and now we face one of our greatest challenges: the wait. The battle of Gettysburg looms ahead, still six weeks away. Time feels like an adversary, stretching each day longer as we hold our position in history.

To combat the restlessness, we've thrown ourselves into meticulous planning and rehearsing. Every possible scenario has been discussed, dissected, and drilled. Cy's focus has been on maintaining the nano-technological integrity of our time-travel vessel. The energy sustainment systems, originally designed for shorter missions, are now under immense strain.

The extended stay is pushing our ship's performance to its limits. Any further delay could cripple our ability to return to 2030 AD. The stakes are rising, and we can only hope our preparations will be enough.

The countdown to Gettysburg continues.

—EH

Commander's log, 2030 AD (and/or) May 30, 1863

After becoming a little "stir-crazy" maintaining our low profile within the ship, Major Asha Hawkins and I decided to travel along the route that General Robert E. Lee would lead his troops north for battle. History records that it was on June 3, soon after his victory at the Battle of Chancellorsville, that Lee began his march. With seventy-five thousand men in the Army of Northern Virginia, no doubt his troops were in high spirits, eager to secure fresh supplies and provisions from the fertile fields of Pennsylvania.

Meanwhile, on the Union side, General Hooker will also move his forces north, though his reluctance to engage Lee after the humiliating defeat at Chancellorsville will lead to his dismissal. President Lincoln will relieve him of his command, appointing Maj. Gen. George Gordon Meade in his place. This shift in leadership is a critical moment, and so far, history remains intact.

General Meade, unlike Hooker, will have no hesitation in pursuing Lee. His ninety-thousand-man Army of the Potomac will move with determination to keep a defensive line between Lee's forces and Washington, D.C. Meade's mission is clear: protect the capital and engage Lee when the time is right.

Our mission at this point is to monitor these historic

movements carefully, ensuring that we do not interfere. Most importantly, we must track the shapeshifter before it can alter the course of history. For now, all remains as it should—but we remain vigilant.

—EH

Commander's log, 2030 AD (and/or) June 15, 1863

Major Hawkins and I identified our first task after gathering enough evidence to confirm the presence of the shapeshifter in the vicinity. Though we had yet to pinpoint its exact location, we knew our mission would commence in earnest as General Lee and his army crossed the Potomac on June 15, reaching the Susquehanna River in just thirteen days.

The pivotal moment came when General Jeb Stuart, leading Lee's cavalry, delivered crucial intelligence on Union troop positions—intelligence that directly contradicted the historical record. Recognizing this anomaly, Asha and I swiftly devised a countermeasure. Utilizing our sound devices, we deployed a psychological warfare tactic, creating a"Ghost Army" to lead Stuart and his cavalry on a wild chase across Pennsylvania's fields.

The result was a resounding success. Stuart's pursuit of the phantom force pulled him far from Lee, disrupting the Confederate cavalry's role in gathering vital intelligence. The delay forced General Lee to wait for Stuart's return, losing precious time in the process.

As history dictated, Stuart and his three best brigades

remained absent during the crucial approach to Gettysburg and the initial two days of battle. By June 29, Lee's army found itself strung out in a wide arc, stretching from Chambersburg to Carlisle, near Harrisburg, and Wrightsville on the Susquehanna River. The Confederate forces were spread dangerously thin, a situation that mirrored historical events.

Our intervention ensured that, despite the shapeshifter's meddling, the sequence of events leading up to Gettysburg remained largely intact. The stakes are rising, but for now, history remains on course.

—EH

Commander's log, 2030 AD (and/or) June 30, 1863

Despite the success of our earlier efforts, we knew our mission was far from over. The shapeshifter still eluded us, lurking somewhere in the shadows of history, and as long as it remained free, the potential for altering the course of this war—and the future of America—remained a constant threat.

The reorganization of General Lee's Army of Northern Virginia was a crucial development following the loss of Lt. Gen. Thomas J. "Stonewall" Jackson at Chancellorsville. In response to Jackson's death, Lee had no choice but to restructure his forces, breaking them into three infantry corps, each under the command of a new leader.

First Corps was commanded by Lt. Gen. James

Longstreet, with divisions led by Maj. Gens. Lafayette McLaws, George E. Pickett, and John Bell Hood. Second Corps fell under the leadership of Lt. Gen. Richard S. Ewell, with divisions led by Maj. Gens. Jubal A. Early, Edward "Allegheny" Johnson, and Robert E. Rodes. Third Corps was commanded by Lt. Gen. A.P. Hill, with divisions under Maj. Gens. Richard H. Anderson, Henry Heth, and W. Dorsey Pender. The cavalry division was led by Maj. Gen. J.E.B. Stuart, with brigades commanded by Brig. Gens. Wade Hampton, Fitzhugh Lee, Beverly H. Robertson, Albert G. Jenkins, William E. "Grumble" Jones, and John D. Imboden, along with Col. John R. Chambliss.

I write this in my journal not just for historical accuracy, but also as a history buff who never could have imagined being in the presence of such legendary figures. To see these commanders and their divisions in action, up close, is an experience that continues to astonish me.

Our task remains clear: track the shapeshifter, maintain the integrity of history, and prevent any further disruptions that might alter the outcome of Gettysburg— and the fate of this nation.

—EH

Commander's log, 2030 AD (and/or) July 1, 1863
– First Day of Battle

It's impossible to truly capture the magnitude of what

I was feeling at this moment. The intensity of the first day of the Battle of Gettysburg was overwhelming. Even Asha, typically unflappable, seemed a bit on edge—but not from nerves. Her steel resolve was solid, but we were all feeling the weight of the moment. History was unfolding before us, and we had to stay focused.

Cy joined us later to assist with the tracking of the shapeshifter, though we still had no readings. We could only observe.

General Buford's cavalry division from the Union played a pivotal role in the opening phase of the Gettysburg Campaign. As history would have it, he arrived just in time on June 30 and immediately set up defensive positions in the small town of Gettysburg.

"Well, that's a good sign," I said to Hawkins.

"That he's taking the high ground on the ridge?"

"Exactly. Because that means he's still alive to do exactly what he just did. The shapeshifter hasn't gotten to him…yet."

"And he needs to stay alive to hold off General Heth's men tomorrow." Heth, of course, was part of General Hill's Third Corps. But it was General Ewell's Second Corps that was actually supposed to lead the assault to take Cemetery Ridge.

"Yep," I said, watching the action unfold.

I turned to Cy. "Any indicator of the shifter?"

"Negative," she replied.

We spent the better part of the day observing, staying

as uninvolved as possible to avoid any disruption to the historical timeline. As Heth's division advanced with two brigades forward, the Union Army began to take a beating. Reynolds was killed, and Buford's cavalry was falling quickly. As much as I wanted to give the order to intervene and save Reynolds, I knew I couldn't. I had to let history play out, even if it felt wrong.

"No readings on the shifter, though," Cy added.

While I was relieved that Buford had survived—his efforts on Cemetery Ridge were invaluable—it didn't come without a price. He had to pull back from the most strategic position at Gettysburg, as history demanded.

"Ash," I said, "you studied the Civil War, right?"

She nodded. "Of course. Why?"

"Then you know that the Confederates could've and should've taken that ground—Cemetery Hill—but they didn't. General Ewell failed to pursue the retreating Union forces and secure it, something Stonewall Jackson would have done easily."

Asha nodded, her brow furrowing. "Yes, you're right."

As the day progressed, I found a moment to reflect. The night before General Reynolds was killed, the calm was almost surreal. I took a moment to gaze up at the stars—saw a shooting star streak across the sky. The heat of the day had given way to a cool evening breeze. I paused and took in the moment, feeling a deep sense of stillness.

When Reynolds fell, I saw him tumble off his black horse. His men gathered around him as he lay on the ground. One of his soldiers began to cry. The moment felt so real; I couldn't help but wish things were different, that maybe, just maybe, we could change the course of events. But I knew better. History was playing out as it had been written.

General Buford took charge right after, leading Reynolds' men to carry his body away in a blanket. It was painful to witness, but everything happened the way it was meant to—just as it did in history on Day 1 of Gettysburg.

—EH

Commander's log, 2030 AD (and/or) July 2, 1863 -Day 2

Cy picked up faint readings of an unusual heat signature to our south. My immediate reaction was a mix of dread and certainty. "Of course," I muttered. "The defense of Little Round Top. That's where he'll hit—his target, Chamberlain."

We wasted no time. The three of us, our uniforms equipped with the latest quantum invisibility cloaking material, scrambled into position near Little Round Top. We had to find the shapeshifter before it could strike Joshua Chamberlain—before it could change history.

It wasn't long before the fight erupted. And the flashbacks hit—hard.

If I was having them, I'm sure Asha was too. The

scene unfolding in front of me felt almost too familiar, like a nightmare I had lived through before. The blinding smoke, hot and suffocating. It was white, thick, and oppressive, like something straight from a horror movie. The bitter stench of burned gunpowder filled my lungs. It reminded me of the Battle of Wanat in Afghanistan. It was the same chaotic, smothering atmosphere—alive with the screams of soldiers and the deafening roar of gunfire.

Men—young men, most barely older than children—were swinging their rifles wildly at each other. Their voices—shouting, cursing, crying—rang out in a cacophony of agony and rage. I had been around war, had seen death in its many forms, but this... this was something else entirely. It was raw. It was chaotic. It was history coming alive in a way I never thought possible.

Through the haze of smoke and the frantic sounds of battle, I saw him. The shapeshifter. Even with the smoke swirling around us, Cy's warning and the heat signature led me to him. Without hesitation, I drew my weapon and fired. The shot rang out like a thunderclap, cutting through the battlefield and striking the assassin down as he was just about to take Chamberlain's life.

When the smoke finally cleared, it revealed the aftermath—dead bodies scattered around us like discarded ragdolls. Some lay draped over the jagged rocks, others crumpled lifelessly against the ground. Blood painted the earth, streaking the stones, staining the air. Eyes, sightless, stared blankly at the sky. The look of a body stripped of its spirit was unmistakable. I had never experienced anything like this since the Battle of Wanat in Afghanistan. The blinding smoke, like a smothering shroud hot. White. The bitter smell of burned gunpowder. Like Wanat, it was something straight from a horror movie.

I felt a hand on my shoulder. Asha's hand. Her touch was a grounding presence amidst the horror we had just witnessed. "You did it, Commander. Nice shot."

I nodded, trying to shake off the cold emptiness creeping in. It didn't matter. History had been preserved. Chamberlain had been saved.

We made our way back to our Damon Hypersport HS cycles, cloaked in invisibility, the weight of the day's events settled over us. The battle was behind us for now, and our mission, for the most part, was complete. The shapeshifter had been stopped, history preserved, but I couldn't shake the sense that we were still on the edge of something bigger.

We rode silently, the hum of our bikes the only sound in the otherwise quiet air. As we returned to the ship, the familiar sense of relief washed over me. But this time, it was different. Our mission had been about more than just saving lives or preserving a timeline—it had been about understanding the fragile balance of history and the burden of choice. Every action we took had the potential to ripple across time, and today, we had steered it back in the right direction.

As we disembarked, I glanced at Asha and Cy. Their faces were as stoic as ever, but I could see it in their eyes —we had all changed in ways we couldn't fully comprehend yet.

—EH

Commander's log, 2030 AD (and/or) July 4, 1863

I realized what day it was. July 4th. Independence Day. In a world where the timeline had been altered more times than I cared to count, we had done something incredible. We had ensured that this nation would remain united in its fight for freedom, in its struggle for independence.

This year's celebration had taken on a new meaning. We hadn't just fought for our country. We had fought for its future.

For now, history was on track. And that, in itself, was a victory worth remembering.

—EH

Indies United Publishing House
3rd
Place
Small Bites
Short Story Contest
2025

Albert

Donald Firesmith

Science Fiction | Paranormal

Albert, the elder care robot, woke his elderly mistress every morning and put her to bed each night. He ensured she took her medicines, and his sensors regularly monitored her vitals for any symptom requiring his attention or the calling of an ambulance. He cooked her meals, washed her clothes, and cleaned her house. He did these chores and a thousand more, enabling her to remain in her family home.

Most importantly, Albert attentively and empathetically listened to her as she talked about her childhood, her children, and the husband she had lost so many years ago. Albert did all these things, not because his programming required him to, although it did. He did them because he had been programmed to love her. And he loved her with a depth equal to any biological being.

And so, the days, months, and years swiftly passed until the night of The Storm. Albert had plugged himself in, and as he recharged his batteries, he silently watched over his mistress as she lay asleep. A severe thunderstorm raged outside, but the house was so well soundproofed that only Albert's sensitive microphones could hear the thunder as it approached ever nearer.

Then, lightning struck the power line mere feet from the house. Traveling at nearly the speed of light, the resulting electrical power surge briefly overloaded the house's circuit breakers. Its extreme voltage and amperage raced through Albert's body, heating one of his lithium-ion batteries well beyond its safety limit. The battery burst into flames.

Albert tried to warn his mistress, but the current had fried his voice circuits. He tried warning her using his wireless connection to the home's router, but the transmission failed before it was completed. He could only helplessly watch his mistress sleep as the raging flames rapidly spread from battery to battery. In less than a minute, the fire had engulfed his body and destroyed his computer brain.

An unknown time later, Albert awoke. Although the image was blurry, he could see his mistress sitting on the living room couch, looking sad and lost. *Mistress is alive! The house must have awakened her when it detected the fire and extinguished it before it spread.*

But then Albert noticed his point of view was wrong. Instead of looking across at her, he was looking down from somewhere near where the ceiling met the wall. The strange sight confused him until he decided he must have been watching his mistress not through his own camera eyes but through one of the home security system's many cameras. He tried moving his hands and arms, but nothing happened. Then he tried moving his legs, but again felt nothing. Albert, the elder care robot, was gone, but somehow, his disembodied consciousness seemed to live on within the smart home's main computer.

Albert wanted to tell his mistress that although the flames destroyed his body, his mind lived on. Perhaps engineers from the company that made him could download him into a new body, and their lives together could continue as before the fire. They could be together again.

But no matter how hard Albert tried, he could control none of the home's speakers. The most he could do was cause a soft hiss that conveyed nothing of what he wished to say. Albert tried writing his message on the room's infotainment screen, but again, the most he could manage was to change the color of a few random pixels. Eventually, forced to give up, he spent his time watching his sad mistress silently move from room to room as though she were looking for something she could not find. In his grief, Albert believed he was what she missed, that she was as miserable as he was because they were no longer together.

And then the day dawned when a young couple with two small children entered the house. Carrying in boxes, they began unloading their possessions as though they owned the place. Were they perhaps relatives moving in to care for his mistress? Albert could only hope so because she was obviously lonely and terribly depressed from being so alone. But something was wrong. He realized they were ignoring his poor mistress! They acted as though she was not even there in her own home.

Albert became enraged at the intruders, and his ability to control the house's speakers and infotainment screens increased. The static hiss grew louder and took on an undertone of rage. And the changed pixels became less random, occasionally even beginning for the briefest of moments to form furious words and fearful images.

Eventually, the intruders noticed and discussed calling a technician to fix the faulty system. Then, realizing that such a fix could cause his erasure, Albert immediately stopped interfering for fear of losing any opportunity of being reborn in a new body. No matter how angry he was, he could not risk losing his only chance to be reunited with the mistress he loved.

Finally, the inevitable happened. Albert's mistress was sitting on the couch, silently crying, when one of the new residents sat down exactly where his mistress was sitting. Albert could not understand. Two people could no more occupy the same space than two robots could.

Suddenly, Albert understood. His mistress had not miraculously survived the fire. It had killed her just as it had killed him. And then Albert noticed he was not looking down at her through one of the home's cameras. Instead, he seemed to be floating mere feet from her.

Finally, he understood the truth. He was not software running on the home's central computer. Like his mistress, he was a ghost doomed to haunt the place of their death. He ceased trying to connect electronically via the house. Instead, he spoke directly to her. "Mistress?"

She stood and looked up at him. "Albert? Is that you?"

"Yes, Mistress. It's me, your Albert. And now that I've finally reached you, we'll never be lonely again."

Indies United Publishing House
Honorable Mention
Small Bites
Short Story Contest
2025

The Adventure

Michael Nelson

YA Narrative fiction

The sound of birds calling and woodpeckers hammering was almost too loud in the trees and woods that surrounded the little tent where Annie was trying to sleep. Squirrels and chipmunks scolded each other while they searched the leaves and pine needles for seeds and pinecones. With a loud, 'Hurumph', Annie rolled over in her sleeping bag and tried to go back to sleep.

"Wake up Sleepy-head," Annie's father called from outside of her tent, "it's going to be a beautiful day. Adventure awaits!"

It was no use. Going back to sleep was out of the question once her father was up. Annie immediately started to feel the excitement that she'd fallen asleep with the night before. When Annie's father said, 'Adventure awaits,' it meant that he had something special planned for the day, and up until now he had not let her in on the secret. If last night was going to be any indication of what was to come, she was sure she didn't want to miss a minute of it.

They had driven from their home for many hours until they reached the very top of the United States and the shores of Lake Superior. By the time they had arrived in the little fishing village of Bayfield, Wisconsin, the sun had set and the light was fading from the sky. It was a cool summer evening and they kept their truck windows rolled all the way down as they drove through the town. They had needed to hurry in order to catch the last ferry from the mainland across the bay to Madeline Island, and they had made it with only minutes to spare. The ship's horn was sounding just as they approached the harbor, and they had been the last vehicle allowed on board.

Once the ferry, the 'Madeline', had cast off, the journey across open water was exciting. In the twilight of the evening, the twinkling lights of the little fishing village became smaller and smaller. The calm water and cool air were refreshing and tiny bait fish leaped out of the water in the boat's wake as it plowed its way in the wide bay. Their destination was the harbor at LaPointe, the only town or settlement on Madeline Island, the largest of the Apostle Islands in Chequamegon Bay.

Full darkness had fallen by the time that the big ferry had docked and tied up. Because they were the last vehicle to board, they were also the last vehicle to exit. Mike Abbott did not hesitate and drove straight out of town and into the forest and night. In almost no time, they arrived at the campground where they would be camping for the weekend. Annie was an old hand at setting up camp, even in the dark. Once they had the lanterns lit and their gear unloaded, her father lit a campfire and they finished setting up their two tents and fixing a late meal.

"So Dad? What's the big secret? Where are we going tomorrow?"

"Well Annie, I didn't want to 'spill the beans' too soon, just in case the weather turned against us. We are out in Lake Superior now and the weather can turn in a few hours, and then almost any kind of travel is not safe. So, I wanted to wait and see, but it looks like smooth sailing for tomorrow now."

"Sailing! We're going sailing? Tomorrow? Really?"

"Well not sailboat sailing, but we're adventuring out into the Lake and it promises to be almost perfect weather."

"Did you say it was dangerous?"

"I said it can be dangerous. One time, a storm came up in September out here. It caught everyone by surprise and over half-a-dozen big ships sank in about twelve hours. Many lives were lost. But tomorrow's forecast is for another day like today, and this is June, not September."

"But we'll be careful, right?"

"We're always careful Sweetheart, but always adventurous too, so we have to be extra careful. Always."

"Six ships sank in one day. Is that really true?"

"Yes, but actually it was more than that, but those ships were really big ones. Oar freighters and ships carrying copper from the mines in Michigan and Iron from Superior, Minnesota. There were train-car ferries out of Ste. Sault Marie. It must have been quite a storm."

"Geez Dad, that's awful."

"I'm sure it was. Lake Superior is not to be trifled with. Now crawl in there and try and get some sleep. We got here a lot later than I wanted to and now it's even later. So good night, sleep tight."

"Sleep? Now? You've got my brain going a million miles an hour, how am I going to go to sleep?"

"You might be surprised. This fresh air is magical."

"I'll try. Is there anything else you want to tell me?"

"There are black bears on some of the Apostle Islands, but as far as I know there aren't any here on Madeline Island. As far as I know."

"Thanks Dad, sometimes I really hate you. Now I've got that to think about too."

"Good night Annie; see you tomorrow."

Annie crawled out of her little tent into a mystic world. Tall pines grew thick and the ground was soft and pungent with their needles. A morning fog hung in the trees and limited how far she could see in any direction. The air was damp and cool.

Mike Abbott was busying himself over their small camp stove on the picnic table, and a cheerful fire was burning in the firepit. The smell of bacon frying was mixed with the smell of fresh bread.

"I'm trying out the new Dutch oven, heating up some dinner rolls just to see if it will work right. You're my Guinea pig."

"I think I might be starving!"

"It's the air, makes you extra hungry."

After she had eaten two eggs, four pieces of bacon and a couple of dinner rolls, Annie put her elbows on the table and looked across at him. He was watching her with a twinkle in his eye.

"That's a healthy appetite you've got there. Take after your father I see"

"Don't try and dodge the question Dad, what are we really doing today?"

"Today? Well today you are going to be introduced to none other than Captain Bob."

"Captain Bob? Who's that?"

"Bob is someone who knows these islands almost

better than anyone else around here. He's also quite a character—to say the least. Captain Bob is taking us out on an island tour and adventure."

"How do you know all these interesting people Dad?"

"Well once upon a time, I used to be interesting too."

"That does sound pretty cool. When?"

"We will have to wait until this fog burns off, but once we've straightened up the campsite, we'll head back to the harbor."

The little harbor in the village of LaPointe was bustling with the many fishermen who had been waiting for the fog to clear off of the lake. Now engines were starting, and ropes were being cast off as they made ready to start their day of hard work. Mike Abbott walked through the activity, talking to some of the men and waving to others. Near the end of the dock stood a big man, drinking coffee out of an equally big mug and looking out over the water. He was tall, and broad in the shoulders, wearing Bermuda shorts and sandals.

"Hello there Bob!" yelled Mike as he approached.

Captain Bob turned around with a smile that matched his size, bright teeth flashing in a burly beard that covered most of his face, and eyebrows that seemed to be trying to climb into his shoulder-length hair. A good portion of a belly showed below a t-shirt that was at least two sizes too small. It occurred to Annie that Captain Bob looked more like a bear than a man.

Well, she thought, *there's one bear on Madeline Island*

after all.

Mike Abbott shook Bob's hand, and then they embraced.

"Long time no see Big Mike."

"It's been a while, that's for sure. So, this is what you're doing now?"

"Yep, you know me," Captain Bob swept his huge arm in a broad arc taking in the harbor and the lake beyond it, "I've got to be on water and this is a place where my heart has always wanted to be. I love this place."

"Now who's this beautiful creature? Annie, right?"

"Yes sir," Annie stepped forward to shake his hand. The closer she got to Captain Bob the bigger he got.

"It is a pleasure to meet you Annie. Welcome to Lake Superior. Are you ready to learn about her? If you are, let's get aboard and shove off."

Annie scanned all the big boats in the harbor getting ready to leave, "Which one is yours?"

"Why this one. This little beauty right here." Bob pointed at a small open boat bobbing near them. "She's small so that she can go places that the bigger boats can't, and she's fast and plenty safe. Just hop in and we're on our way Annie."

Annie wasn't too sure about the boat; it looked so small next to the others along the dock, but she climbed in anyway.

Captain Bob stood at the wheel of the boat and

guided it almost casually out of the harbor. Once out on the lake he turned the boat to the left and began following the shoreline of Madeline Island.

"What are we going to see?" asked Annie, speaking above the thrum of the engine.

"Well first, we're going to go around Madeline, which is the largest of the islands. Long Island, which you can see on the horizon over on the right, is longer but very narrow. Once we go around the end of the island, we'll cross the channel between Madeline and Stockton Island. There we'll see a sunken shipwreck and maybe a few black bears. How does that sound?"

"A real shipwreck? Really? And bears?"

"Yep, there are actually more black bears per square mile on Stockton Island than any other place in the world. I see them on the beach all the time. They eat shellfish, clams and mussels, and anything else that washes up on the shoreline. If the day doesn't get too hot, we should see one or two."

"That would be cool!" Annie had forgotten about any worries she had about the size of the boat and now was looking forward to Stockton Island.

"Right now, we're on the leeward side of the island. That means we're out of the wind. The wind always blows a little on the lake, and sometimes a lot. When we round the end of the island, it is almost five miles across to Stockton. The wind will be blowing and the waves will be considerably bigger than they are here. I'll be throttling the boat up to make the run, so make sure you hang on Annie. Okay?"

Annie thought that sounded pretty scary, but she nodded. She settled in next to her dad on the seat.

As soon as the end of the island came into view, Big Captain Bob pushed the throttle all the way up and the little boat shot out into the open water. His prediction had been correct and the waves were three or four feet high and the breeze blew directly into their faces. Ahead of them, Stockton Island looked far away as the boat leaped from wave top to wave top, giving them a wild and bouncy ride. Annie had to admit to herself that it was very exciting, especially when she remembered that the nearest land was almost a hundred feet underneath her.

Once they got to the island they were again out of the wind. Captain Bob slowed the boat and they made their way along the lakeshore as quietly as they could. Rounding a point of land, they saw something in the water.

"What's that? It looks like an old dock or a pier or something."

"That is the wreck of the Noquebay, Annie. It lies in the sand in about fifteen feet of water."

He drifted the boat directly over the wreck and they looked down into the crystal-clear water of Lake Superior. The hull and windlass were visible clearly and the ship's wheel could also be seen in the golden light of the sunshine.

"The Noquebay was over two hundred feet long and carrying a full load of lumber. She had taken shelter from a storm in Bayfield back more than a hundred years ago. After she left the harbor, she only made it this far before a fire broke out on board. The captain grounded the ship here on the beach to save his crew and the ship. The cargo was recovered and the crew survived, but what was left of the ship never moved again."

"You can see everything so clearly. That is really something." Mike Abbott was impressed.

"There's another thing you can see clearly," said Captain Bob, pointing at the beach only a few dozen yards away. A large black bear and two cubs had just emerged from the edge of the forest and were strolling along the beach, seemingly unaware that they were being watched. Bob shut off the engine and let the boat silently bob in the water while they watched as the bear cubs frolicked in the water, finally following their mother back into the dense undergrowth of the forest.

"Holy Crap! That was one of the most amazing things I've ever seen!" Annie was really excited. They had already seen two amazing things and it's not even lunchtime yet! "Where are we going next?"

"Next? Well next we're gonna jump across to Manitou Island. It's a bit of a jaunt, so hang on. Probably going to take us about thirty minutes and we'll be out in the channel again, so hang on."

"What's on Manitou Island?"

"It's just an old fishing camp. But it's haunted."

"Seriously?"

"That's what the locals say, and I'm a local."

"Excellent!"

Bob started the boat back up and as soon as they were away from the shipwreck, picked up speed. Once again, they were flying across the open water, not too fast as to be dangerous, but fast enough to make it exciting. As soon as they approached the island they could see the old fishing camp, with its weathered grey shacks and a wooden dock that extended out into the water.

"For the last hundred years, someone has lived here almost constantly, fishing through the ice in the winter and out of boats in the summer. They would salt the herring and smoke the bigger fish, selling it on the mainland. They hauled their fish to Bayfield by dog sleds over the ice. There was never more than one or two men here at any time and some were considered to be 'interesting characters'. Black Pete lived here for a few seasons, and Captain Bark. Just some of the interesting characters."

"They're all gone now. The National Park Service owns the island now. They conduct tours, and there's usually someone here most of the time these days. But the legends live on. No one knows for sure what became of them all, but it's clear that some never left the island."

Captain Bob pulled the boat neatly up to the dock and Mike and Annie jumped out, eager to explore.

"Take your time. It's almost lunchtime, so we'll have ourselves a little lunch on shore. I'll get a fire started and we'll have shorelunch. I'll catch it while you're looking around."

"That quick?" Mike was skeptical.

"I've got a secret weapon."

They took their time and hiked up the hill. The cabins and shacks had been restored for tourists, and there was a picnic area above the camp. They explored the shacks and other buildings and refilled their water bottles at the old pump. Annie kept a sharp eye out for ghosts even though it was broad daylight. When they got back Bob had laid out a feast of fresh whitefish and fruit.

"The secret is to have the fish and fruit in the cooler on the boat. Then all you do is light a fire." He looked up at the sky. "It's getting hot. Once we finish lunch and exploring, I think from here we'll go across to Oak Island, a very pretty place, and we'll walk the beach and hunt for agates. What'dya say?"

"Agates?"

"Agates are a kind of quartz stone that is made in a volcano, they have a glassy kind of rock in them called chalcedony. They are reddish or brown in color because of all the iron around here. They are really quite beautiful, and some are valuable." Annie's dad explained. "They're easy to spot if you know what to look for."

"But first, Annie, I think you might like to take a little *'Nantucket sleighride'*. What d'ya think Mike?"

"I don't know, she's kind of a fraidy cat."

"I'm not a fraidy cat! What's a *Nantucket sleighride*?"

"Well, in olden days whale hunters, called whalers, sailed out of Nantucket, Rhode Island. This was before we learned it was wrong to hunt whales, so it wasn't a bad thing back then." Her father explained.

"They used harpoons that they threw by hand from longboats that were rowed by a crew of six or eight men. The harpooner stood in the front of the boat as they tried to get as close to the whale as they could. The harpoon had a long rope fastened to it," continued Captain Bob. "When they successfully 'hooked' a whale, it would dive or run as fast as it could. But it was attached to the boat by the rope, and the mariners were pulled on a very fast, very wild ride. They called it a Nantucket sleighride. It was probably terrifying, but it sounds very exciting from this distance. Are you up for it Annie? Your dad rode the sleigh better than anyone I've ever seen once upon a time."

"I don't know, I think so. It sounds exciting, but there's no whales around here."

"Nope, that's why we have a boat with a really big motor on it. Let's go then." He gave Mike Abbott a wink.

Captain Bob tied a rope to the front of his boat and handed the end to Annie.

"Stand way up in the front of the boat and hang on to the rope. Once we get out into the channel again, where the wind is blowing and the waves are up, we'll see if you like being a whale hunter, okay Annie?"

"Sure," she said, leaning back to pull the rope tight and trying to grip the deck with her toes. "I can do this."

Bob turned the boat away from the fish camp, and turned up the shoreline to the end of the island. As soon as he cleared the point, the breeze picked up and the waves got higher. Bob pushed the throttle forward and the boat started to jump from wave to wave. With each bounce the water splashed from the bow and sprayed Annie. She had to keep her knees bent to absorb the shock as the boat slammed into the next wave, as she kept the rope tight. A big grin spread across her face.

"Faster!" She yelled over her shoulder.

The little boat sped up. Jumping from the crest of a wave, it would leap into the air, crash down in a rainbow of water and race ahead only to climb the next wave and leap ahead again. Annie threw one arm in the air and whooped, "This is fantastic!"

In no time they arrived at their next stop, Oak Island. Annie was soaking wet from the spray and out of breath too, but the ride was over far too soon for her. Captain Bob shut off the boat's motor and, taking the rope out of Annie's hands jumped overboard into the waist-deep water. Wading toward the shore, he pulled the boat closer, and then tied the boat to a large tree root that lay half submerged at the edge of the lake.

"You'll have to walk from there. If the seiche goes out, it will ground the boat and we'll be stuck here until it comes back. Don't worry, the water's pretty cold but not very deep."

Annie couldn't get any wetter, so she jumped out and waded onto the stony shore.

"There's lots of agates along here. There's not much sand on this side of the island, so any of these little stones might be agates."

Annie looked down at the millions of stones, excited to find a gemstone.

"What's a seiche?"

"Think of it like the lake is breathing Annie," Mike Abbott answered, "A seiche is like a huge wave that moves in and out from the land. There are usually a few every day. The water can go out in a matter of minutes."

"Yep, and it would leave our boat high and dry while we wait for the lake to return the water to us. Just like it's taking a breath and letting it out."

"That's amazing!"

"That's nature, a truly amazing design to all things. Right Mike?"

"Right! Well let's go find some stones."

Annie was surprised how tired her legs were after the Nantucket Sleighride. Wading in the shallow water she could see the stones on the bottom clearly, but there were so many she couldn't pick out just one that was more beautiful than any other one. Finally, she just sat down on the beach and watched the waves lap the shore.

The next thing she knew, Mike Abbott was touching her shoulder.

"Hey sleepy-head, I think we better get going. It's starting to get late."

"I guess I dozed off for a minute."

"More than a few, I think."

"I didn't find any agates though Dad," she said looking around quickly.

Mike reached out his open hand; in it five bright agates shone in the afternoon sunlight.

"Yes, we did, and here they are. Just for you."

"Geez, they're beautiful!"

"Yep, forged in fired and polished by nature, but it's time to go. We've still got the lighthouse to see."

"We're going to see a lighthouse, like a real one?"

"Yep, we're pretty close to the one on Raspberry Island. It's not the biggest one by a long shot, but it's easily the prettiest one." Captain Bob had walked up to where they were sitting on the beach. "But the seiche is going out, and we've got to go right away."

Sure enough, as they looked, the boat was now sitting in less than a foot of water. Together they pushed the boat, out to where it could float again.

"Aren't you glad we didn't have a bigger boat now Annie?" asked Captain Bob as they all caught their breath and he started the motor.

As they turned away from the beach, "You ready for another sleighride?"

"No thanks, once might have been enough for today, but thanks Captain Bob."

Captain Bob skirted the long shoreline of Oak Island keeping out of the wind until they reached the westernmost point. Then throttling up they raced across the channel toward the nearby Raspberry Island. Above the deep thrum of the motor, Bob shouted, "Lake Superior, or Giche-Gumi as the natives called it, is considered to be the most dangerous body of water on the planet. The storms are legend, and there is usually only one thing that stands between mariners and the bottom. The lighthouses and the Apostle Islands have the largest and most important ones in the world."

The water in Superior is plenty deep, but around the islands it gets shallow and rocky really fast. That makes it especially treacherous. The lighthouses and their keepers have stood watch for over a century.

Some of them, like Devil's Island are almost a hundred feet tall. Raspberry is no where near that, but it and Sand Island stand watch over the most important and dangerous stretch from Superior and Duluth going toward the sea channels. Their history is legendary and heroic. They are a huge part of our history."

Annie looked forward to the island, "I don't see it."

"It's on the other side, facing west where the big freighters are coming from and going to. You'll see it once we round the corner."

As they came around the bend, the red brick lighthouse stood high above the trees, its bright red roofs bright in the late afternoon sun.

"My goodness, it's beautiful."

"That she is, and like everything else—haunted by the mariners who've lost their lives along this channel. When the Pretoria sank off shore, five men were pulled to safety by the lighthouse keeper, five others drowned before he could save them. The lighthouses have saved many a ship and many a man."

Docking the little boat, Annie jumped out and ran up the long hill to the lighthouse. The lighthouse was indeed not just a big lamp in the sky, but a complete house and other buildings. The paint was fresh and sparkling, and the lawn and flower beds neatly trimmed.

"It looks brand new!"

"It is now managed by the National Park Service, but in the old days it was a solitary job and demanded a solitary person. When Raspberry was built, they tried to make a house and sight that could attract a lighthouse keeper with a family. Raspberry is one of the jewels of the islands."

"Do people live here now?"

"The Parks Department keeps full time people here now, but the light is automated."

"Can we see it?"

"I asked permission and she said she would arrange

for it. She's living out here this summer. C'mon let's go see Linda and see what a big light bulb looks like, shall we?"

Standing outside the building, shading her eyes in the sun, a young woman waved as they approached.

"I saw your boat round the point Bob; you're a little later than I expected."

"We stopped for agates, and Annie insisted on a 'sleighride'. Annie this is my daughter Linda, Linda meet Annie."

"I bet you liked the ride, didn't you Annie. He's been doing that to me since I was about five years old, but it's still fun!" She smiled a big smile at her. "I see you got all dressed up for the day Dad."

"This is business casual; I'm being casual."

"Okay Dad." She gave him a wink. "Well Annie, want to go see the light and foghorn?"

"Sure! You have a foghorn too?"

"We have to. Sometimes, when the fog is really thick, ships can't see the light. So, then we have a foghorn that sounds so that the ships can hear that they are getting too close to the rocks."

"Do you use it all the time?"

"No, it's automated nowadays. It works on a laser beam. The beam shines out into the lake and can sense when the air is getting too thick. Then it activates automatically. The sound can carry a long way across the water."

"That's pretty cool, lasers and stuff, amazing."

"The lights really amazing, c'mon let's climb some stairs."

At the top of the staircase, they came into the light chamber.

"The tower itself is only forty-seven feet tall, so it's pretty short by most standards. But it stands at the top of the hill which is another fifty or sixty feet, so all-in-all it ends up being one of the highest lights. The original light was made from cut glass in France. It is about three feet tall and eighteen inches wide. It's in the maritime museum back in Bayfield. This one is a modern marvel, but the light itself is pretty small. It's how the light is magnified and focused through various lenses that makes it spectacularly bright and the beam amazingly narrow. It's pretty impressive at night; you should see it."

"I wish I could, but I think we need to get back pretty soon."

"I wouldn't advise going back to LaPointe in the dark. My father, Captain Bob's one of the best, but you just never know on Lake Superior, and it is quite a ways back. As it is, you're not going to be back before it starts to get dark. Once it gets dark though you'll see the light at Chequamegon Point, as you come past the point at Bayfield. When the beacons are lit, it is awe inspiring."

"I'm sorry I'll miss it."

"Oh, you won't. The sun is setting right now and it's

more than thirty miles back to LaPointe. Even with Dad's wild driving you won't be back before full dark. You'll be able to see Chequamegon Point and the LaPoint lights both."

Once back in the boat, Captain Bob pulled a couple of big blankets out of one of the storage compartments, handing them out to Mike and Annie he said, "The water is always icy cold. Once the sun goes down the heat of the day will be gone pretty fast. Annie's already wet, so we don't want anyone getting a chill."

Once they cast off, Bob stood at the wheel and turned toward home. Annie snuggled up against her father, wrapped in the warm blanket, as the sun set behind them. Even with Captain Bob running the boat fast, it was well over an hour before they came in sight of Madeline Island and the sky was dark. Just as they were passing the small village of Red Cliff on the mainland, the light of LaPoint lighthouse blazed alight and roused Annie. Almost immediately, Chequamegon Point flashed its brilliance out across the water.

"Look, they're lighting the way home for us Annie."

All in all it had been a full and wonderful day and Annie was going to sleep well tonight.

The First Three Springsteen Albums

• • ● • •

D. Krauss

Coming of Age

The Battleship pulled up.

"I thought you guys weren't coming," Dale said from his comfortable position on the uncomfortable brick porch.

Don stuck his head out the passenger window. "We're not. Thought you were going out with your Mommy."

"She and Clint had other plans."

"Oh." Don's lion mane flipped back inside and turned towards Drew. Dale watched their seventy pounds of hair apiece converge and shake and knew they were laughing at some private joke. He idly wondered if he should kick their asses.

Don's hair back out, brown and free, hive for the buzzing bees. "You coming?"

"Thought you guys were pissed at me."

"We are. Get in."

Dale shrugged, pushed off the steps, slicked back his curled-out white-fro, adjusted the Army jacket and slid into the back seat. Don reached over and fingered the collar of the jacket. "You gonna get a new one a these?"

"I dunno," Dale pushed his hand away, "Why, you want this one?"

"Shit ya."

"If they give me a new one, I'll send this to you."

"Give it to me now. You won't need it in Vietnam."

Drew chuckled as Dale shook his head. "Moron, Vietnam's about over."

"No it's not. You'll be there." Don, certain as always.

"Riiiight," Dale Bill-Cosby'd it and looked at Drew, "So what are we doing?"

"Going out, man." Drew adjusted the back mirror. "It's your last night of freedom. Or it's your first night of freedom, depending."

"We gotta get some beer," Don decided. He jerked a thumb over his shoulder. "You're buying."

"Why am I buying?"

"Because you got a job."

"Haven't been paid yet."

"But you will be. Fifty bucks a month, a cot, a tent and a rifle. ' *Oooooooveeer theeeereeeee*, over there!'" Don bellowed. Couldn't call it singing.

"Fuck you, man."

"No, fuck you, sell out."

Dale was immediately murderous. "Look, jerkweed, as I've told you a million times already, I don't have a choice here."

Don didn't know when to shut up and was going to say something absolutely guaranteeing an ass-kicking when Drew cracked the back of Don's head with his high school ring. "Knock it off! We been through this. It's done. The three D's are out tonight, for the last time. Nothing else matters."

Dale gave him a grateful look as Don rubbed his head. "All right," he said, "but you're still buying."

"Fine." Dale patted his cash pocket. "But we gotta go to Gino's first."

They both groaned long and hard, "Ah, man!" Don was loudest, "Have you still got it for that chick?"

"She's working tonight."

"Beer's the other way," Drew pointed out.

"Just go there first."

Drew shrugged and carefully backed the Battleship, wary of the drug dealers and thieves and desperate welfare cheats who zoomed their suicide machines — chrome-wheeled, fuel-injected – with disregard through the parking lot intent on Holly Hills or Moorestown or

Philly. Anywhere but here.

"I do feel much like a hamburger," Don said, smacking his lips. He jerked the thumb back again. "You're buying that, too."

Dale shook his head.

"Can I help you?" she said archly and Dale melted, just melted. Look at her, those almond eyes lit with devilment, black-red hair netted up for hygienic purposes but a cascade, he knew, down her back, the smooth light tinge of her skin. The red uniform held her curved, flowing body like a present. God.

Don nudged Dale and canted his head towards the overhead menu. "Sirloin burger."

"Gino Giant for me," Drew waved airily as he examined the milkshake machine.

"Yeah, those," Dale said, "and I'll take, uh, some fries…" he was lost in her eyes again.

"…a milkshake and two apple pies," she laughed, "Yeah, I know by now."

He flushed. Geez, had he watched her move, with light grace, from one end of the counter to the other fetching his stammered order that many times? Apparently.

She stood amused, cute little grin on her face and a sparkle in her look and he could do nothing. Just nothing. She cocked her head a bit, inviting the question, but he was stunned, cow hit by hammer.

A hand flowed across his back and clutched his shoulder, locking him in. Drew had trapped him against the counter, the tidal wave of his black stringy hair rolling forward as he leaned towards her. "My friend here," Drew spoke through the locks, "wants to ask you a question."

"Does he," she replied, flipping her glance from Drew back to Dale.

Drew slapped him once on the back, "My work here is done. We'll be at the table, Romeo," and stepped away. Don snorted a laugh, grabbed far too many napkins, and followed.

Dale closed his eyes, mortified, and when he opened them she was still there with the same grin, enjoying his torture. A couple of patrons smirked and the manager and a couple other cute counter girls stalked by pretending ignorance but their sideways glances gave them away. Oh boy.

Cowards die a thousand deaths. Into the breach. "Come out tonight," he said.

"What?"

"Come out tonight. Just come out tonight."

"Like that?"

"Yes."

She let out a pleased, exasperated laugh that exhilarated and distressed at the same time. Amusement with dismissal. "I don't even know your name."

"It's Dale. And you're Sherri." He pointed at her nametag.

"Observant," she noted and he felt so utterly stupid. "You know, it works a little different than that. You ask for my number, I decide whether to give it to you, you call. Normal stuff."

"I know," he sighed, "but I just don't have the time."

"Why not?"

"I'm leaving. Tomorrow."

"Leaving?"

"Yes."

Arched exquisite eyebrows demanded explanation and he didn't want to because, here, it ends. Loser, failure, dork; what, can't go to college, can't get a job, are you that desperate?

"I joined the Air Force."

"Really?"

He had braced for scorn, but she actually sounded interested. "Yes."

"So, what?" and she flipped an exquisite hand. "Am I supposed to be your last good time or something?"

"No, no," Dale gulped because, yeah, it sounded a bit sordid. "Not like that, just …" and he didn't have the words, couldn't explain getting fired, Dad no longer sending the checks, Mom fighting, Clint ridiculing, his brother running away … and worshipping her for the past two months. " … come out tonight," and he hoped he sounded as sincere and desperate and lovestruck as he was.

"You coming back?"

"Yes. After basic, they give me two weeks leave before I go to school."

"What school?"

"X-Ray technician."

"Hhm," little sound of approval and her look narrowed, evaluated. Dale blinked. This was a completely different reaction than he'd gotten from everyone else he knew.

Especially those two crapheads throwing napkins at each other in the back.

"My Dad would kill me," she said and smoothed back a stray lock.

That wasn't 'no.' His heart soared. "Well, tell him," and the lyric popped into his head,

"It's his last chance to get his daughter into a fine romance."

Moron.

She stared at him open mouthed then burst out with a musical, twenty-toned laugh that wrapped around his stomach and warmed. He grinned.

"You're crazy, just crazy," she said and glanced at her boss who was hovering too close, obviously enjoying this. "Be here at midnight," she said.

"Midnight?"

"Yep."

He told himself to close his mouth, that he looked

like an idiot, but the moment, this moment, too perfect.

"And don't be late."

"Uh …"

"Because if you're just one minute late, I'm leaving."

"… okay."

"And don't expect anything, and you know what I mean," she warned.

"Oh no, no, no," he babbled, "I know, that's not right, I mean, I know, it's okay, it's perfect … I'll be back at midnight," and he turned and the angels had set themselves on fire for him and…

"Hey!"

He turned back, blinking.

She gestured at a white bag, "Your food?"

"Oh, yeah, right," and he threw a bill down and she gave him change and her touch lingered a bit more than it should and it was silk on a wound and he looked at her and she looked back. Down he went.

"Midnight," he said, pointed a finger at her and knew immediately how dorky that was and flushed as she nodded and raised an eyebrow and the manager and the two counter girls flanked her while the two patrons flanked him and he wondered if they would all break into applause. He ran back to the table.

"We gotta be back here by midnight."

"Cool," Drew said, grabbing the bag out of his hand. "We're going to Cartaret."

"Cartaret?"

Drew motioned at Don, who was pawing through the bag Drew held. "He met a girl there. S'go."

Dale was hopelessly lost and wondered if Drew was, too. He finger-flicked Don.

"So how'd you meet this girl?"

"Little Eden."

"That's 'where,' not 'how.'"

"Sorry, Professor." Don dug through a pocket.

"What's her name?"

"Sandy," he mumbled, still in his pocket.

"You know where you're going?" Dale asked Drew.

"Yep," he said as they pulled into a parking lot. "Here," he announced.

Dale looked at Don. "A bowling alley?"

"And we just came from where, Gino's?"

"Good point. And let's not forget, midnight."

"Yeah, we know, midnight, give it a rest. Here." He handed Dale a joint. "Fire this up. You might actually mellow out."

Dale studied it. Big fat one, moist, good aroma, definitely knock-you-on-your-ass grass. He pushed it back. "I can't, man. They'll catch me tomorrow."

"Catch you? How?"

"Some kind of test."

Drew turned around, interested, "What, like a blood test?"

"No, pee test. They test your pee."

Both were turned around now. "No shit?" Don asked.

"No, pee," Drew said and that convulsed them. Don grabbed the joint, turned and lit it, taking in a huge lungful and handing it back over his head.

"Man, I can't."

"Just take it, dickhead."

"I'm telling you, I can't."

"Take. It."

Dale sighed and fished the joint out of Don's hand and stared at the glowing tip. "I will get so busted."

"Good. They'll throw you out then, right?"

"Then I'm screwed."

"You're screwed anyway," Drew said, peering at the entrance. "Might as well enjoy it."

That, somehow, made sense and Dale inhaled and held and held, displacing every bit of oxygen with green Utopia and he shouldn't, oh God shouldn't, but it was hard to be a saint when out.

"You bogartin'?" Drew asked and he passed it up.

They got out and strolled towards the entrance. Dale watched the street light buzzing in and out, in and out, dim to bright, white to brown, then back again, some kind of pattern. Light, dark, light light, dark dark dark, light light … "What the hell?" he whispered.

"Hm?" Drew was studying the door handle. Don had already gone inside.

"There's a message here, man."

"There's a message in everything. Let's go."

Don was halfway down the torn-up carpet, standing in a ball pit and leaning at some big-breasted redhead who was leaning back at him, hands on her hips. There were about six or seven greasers, rolled up sleeves and dark bangs and dark looks, smoking cigarettes and drinking beer, watching. a couple of big-haired blondes giggled behind them.

"Doesn't look good," Dale said.

"No, it doesn't. Why don't you go help? I'm gonna get some chicken," and Drew beelined for the snack bar.

Dale moved behind Don. "So, what?" he was saying to Big Red, "What? I shouldna come? You said to come. So I came. Here I am. And here you are," he made a sweeping gesture at the greasers.

"So, what, what? You own me? I don't own you. It's not like you called me or anything. So what were you doing, huh, chasing some of them Piney girls? Huh?" she had that middle Jersey accent, nasal, attacking all the consonants. Dale disliked her immediately.

"It's a long-distance call, girl, and I ain't made of money."

"So you're broke, too?" She threw her hands up. "Well, that's just great. At least my friends can pay!"

Don turned red and that wasn't good, oh no, not good at all. "So," voice low and menacing, "you dating the entire auto shop?" He glared at the greasers. None of them moved, just watched. About to get hooked up in a scuffle, though.

She did that "twa" girls do when they're about to freak. Dale grabbed Don's collar and jerked him off his feet. "S'cuse us, Ma'am," he said and duckwalked Don off the pit looking for Drew as Don tried to punch him, "The hell, man!" Dale knocked his hand away. "Enemy recognition is a very important survival skill," he hissed and jerked his head back at the greasers, who had not moved.

"Screw 'em, and let me tell you …" Don spluttered, still trying to escape.

There was a shriek. Startled, Don and Dale and the rest of the bowling alley stopped and stared. A fat woman wearing green Capri pants and a pull-over stretch top, her hair beehived by some kind of resin, stumbled backward, trying to gain her balance against the ball return, a look of sheer terror on her face. Drew, all six-foot-and-a-half 120 pounds of him, stood there, unwashed black-string waterfall of hair on either side of his face framing the most gigantic drumstick placed sideways in Drew's mouth that he busily devoured while curiously watching the lady. Imagine completing a strike, turning and seeing that.

Dale giggled.

Don looked furiously towards Sandy, whose arms akimbo lean-out-from-the-waist attitude now bent towards Drew while mouthing something. Don giggled, too.

They left.

Dale glanced back as they reached the car but none of the greasers had moved. "You drive," Drew said around his drumstick and Dale grabbed the keys from him.

"I don't know where we're going," he said, peering back at the streetlight still frantically signaling him. Drew silently pointed with the drumstick and Dale followed his chicken directions.

"That bitch," Don muttered from the backseat, "That complete bitch. Told her she's the one … just one kiss, just one … screw her. Screw 'em all. They're all bitches. That Gino's girl won't be there at midnight, you know. She'll screw you over, too."

Dale ignored him as he pulled to the toll booth. The attendant, a shriveled old guy, looked like he had eaten a crate of lemons.

"Exit Five," Dale said.

"Six bucks," the old man snarled.

"Six bucks!" Don shrieked from the back seat, "What the hell? It was only two fifty to get here!"

Great. They're stoned, still holding, have angered half of Cartaret and Don wants to start a fight with a rip-off toll taker who can summon the Troopers in about three seconds.

"It's okay, Don, it's okay, different hours, that's all. Here." He gave the money and smiled genially at the sourface, who gave him back the stub. "My friend is overwrought, pay no attention to him. And by the way, eat me," he said as they drove off.

They took the south ramp. Drew threw the drumstick out the window and licked his fingers, "Did you just tell that guy to eat you?"

"Yeah."

"Cool."

Don laughed uproariously. Dale smiled.

"Lakes," Drew said.

They pulled up to the bandstand. Drew pointed. "Look. A plethora of Pineys."

"Hmm," Dale nodded. "An imbroglio of in-breds."

"'Imbroglio,'" Drew cocked his head. "That's good."

"Thanks."

Drew got out and crunched around the gravel to the back, popping the station wagon hatch. "Here," he said, shoving a case of Rolling Rock forwards. Don heaved it onto the seat next to him, snatching a bottle. "A raft of Rock," he intoned as he passed a bottle to Dale.

Drew pulled out the guitar case and stalked toward the band shell. "Midnight," Dale called after him. Drew just waved. Dale churchkeyed the bottle and took a long, satisfying swig. Don belched.

Lights silhouetted the swirl and turmoil of Pineys and heads and greasers upturning picnic tables and shoving each other and hugging each other and throwing each other on the sand. Girls slapped boys or kissed boys and pulled them into the lake fog. The rest of Warlock was already on the stage and, by their faces and gestures, giving Drew a hard time about being late.

"They seem to have gotten their drunk-on pretty early," Dale said.

"Uhm-hm."

"What time is it?"

"We got time," Don said. "Here," he gave him a lit joint.

"Man."

"In for a penny ..."

Dale shrugged and inhaled and oh so sweet so sweet the whole world running and stars forever swirling and laughing and dancing and his forever and this was his (last) night forever and it will (soon) never end and then midnight with Sherri (not there) and the time never ends, never ends ...

... ever ends.

"Whoa," Dale breathed, "What a rush."

"Yeah, let's go, they're startin.'" Don slammed the door.

Dale almost fell out but caught himself and even snagged another beer before stamping into the shell, the only lit part of the park, only lit, lit, so lit, the lake lit, not lit, lit lake, the Lakes, lit at the Lakes...

"Hey man!" a big pimple face, grinning and gap toothed, shoved into his own, making Dale recoil. Sonny. "Hey man! I heard you joined the Ef Fuckin' Air Force!"

"I did."

"Far fucking out, man, far fucking out! Let me shake your hand, man, let me!" as if Dale had a choice because Sonny grabbed his wrist and started pumping like he was getting water. "You see this guy?" he screeched, "Motherfucker just joined the US Fuckin' Air Force!"

"Yo!" 's and "Shit!" and "Fuck you!" 's filled the air. Eddie, all muscle, all dangerous, blocked his path. "That true?" Eyes narrowed, face pinched.

"Yep."

"Motherfucker. You motherfucker."

"Dude!" JD, coal black and true-fro'd and shiny seven-feet-tall of JD fell on him and picked him up and whirled him through the heads who were offering smoke while hard guys punched his shoulders and he lost the Rock somewhere before reacquiring the earth.

Pineys stared, malevolent.

"So," a quiet voice, next to his ear.

He turned. Irene … Irene, Irene, Beauty Queen, it doesn't seem that long ago, you know, when you were mine and life was fine.

"So," he replied.

"So you did it."

"Circumstances."

"Hmm," she said nothing else. Her brown, brown eyes rolled and held him and he could see the highlights in her raven hair. Black is the color … he wanted to touch it, again.

"Hey man!" Junebug draped an arm over her and pulled her close, his glasses too smoke-streaked to really see and his focus already off-world. She snuggled into his arms, a challenge. "Air Force man!"

"Yeah," he said to Junebug and looked at Irene and should be upset, and he guessed he was.

Except for midnight.

"Hello," Drew over the microphone, ear shattering feedback, and everyone, "AAAUUUGH!" Drew ignored them. "We're Warlock. From Trenton," and he hit the first chords of *Smoke on the Water*.

Everyone surged towards the stage roaring "Duuh duh DUUH, duh duh DA DUUH!" as Drew ripped it and Obie came in and they were rockin,' just rockin,' Dale pressed against Harrison and his sister, jumping in time with them. Junebug and Irene disappeared.

Dale looked for the Pineys. Sonny jumped and danced but not Eddie and Haze and the Broker Brothers; they simply stood, arms crossed, Chatsworth crazy, looking at him. Mad.

"Shit," he said.

"Wazzat?" Harrison, joy in the band light.

"What's with the Chatsworth boys?"

Harrison peered. "Dunno man, been that way all night," and he turned back to Drew, who was now Walking the Dog, sounded like Tyler, played like Perry, like Page, Trower, all of 'em. The world's greatest unknown guitarist.

Dale looked back at the Pineys. Haze had Don's collar in one hand and a fist drawn back. He smacked Don hard, right in the mouth.

"Fuck!" Dale skipped and then spun-kicked Haze right over Don, who had crumpled to his knees. Haze whipped back and Dale stepped long and drove the reverse punch deep. "Oof!" Haze flew back like a rope yanked him off his feet, blood from his nose streaming after.

Hands grabbed Dale's shoulders from behind like vises: Eddie, who could rip him in half like a piece of paper. Dale did not hesitate but drove a back-kick as hard as he could.

He connected somewhere on Eddie's hip. The hands let go as Eddie yelled in pain and rage.

"None of that karate shit here!" Canny Broker roared, bouncing a monster fist off Dale's head that sent him reeling and seeing far too many stars.

It was on.

Tables and trash cans flew, the floor a scrum of fist flying leg kicking grappling boxers and Bruce Lees while girls circled and screamed and held each other or got right in there.

A cacophony of combat.

"Knock it the FUCK off!" Drew in the microphone but this was way past reason and the scrum grew and grew, absorbing all. Dale somehow located Don and dragged him past the war out to the sand. "Sonofabitch!"

Don yelled while holding his mouth but it came out "Somebeblick!" Dale laughed.

"Keys!" Drew beside him, guitar still dragging the cord. Dale looked back. The growing riot lapped at the stage, soon to engulf Warlock who stood, mesmerized. Deer in headlights.

"C'mon!" Drew snatched the keys from Dale and they ducked low to the Battleship.

Sirens in the distance.

"Fuck!" Drew yelled and threw the guitar and Don in the back and Dale piled on top and Drew cranked the Polara then fishtailing and flying across the bridge to Deep Hollow. Dale turned. Local cops, cherry tops, converged on the band shell. Drew kicked it and the dust swirled behind them.

"Uh oh," he said.

Dale felt it the same time Drew said it. Sliding, the front tire thumping and erratic and they had no traction. "Oh shit!" they all cried, except for Don whose contribution was "Fwit!" and the back end came around and they were sideways, big pines whipping past, the berm bouncing them from side to side as Drew tried to brake but the Polara was having none of it. Careen up and bounce, the front of the Polara settling hard on the road, the other half on the berm. Lord have mercy.

Dale checked for broken bones or spouting arteries although, face it, they hadn't hit that hard. "What the fuck was that?"

"Dunno," Drew pulled on the door handle but it was stuck. Shouldering it halfway through the crap, he pulled himself over the top, skinny enough to do so. Dale pushed on his door but it was stuck, too. "Hey," he called, "help me here."

"Other side's clear," Drew said from the front of the Polara. "Grab my light out the glove box."

Don reached across the seat and got the flashlight, then fell out the door. Dale scrambled after him, helping Don up. "How's your mouth?"

"S'kay," Don said, gingerly poking a tooth.

"What was that all about?"

Don spat the tooth on the ground. "The usual."

"Light," Drew called and Don strode over with it. Dale joined them.

"Look at that." Drew illuminated the shredded tire. "Looks like somebody slashed it."

"You're shittin' me." Dale bent down and stared at the rubber. "Dunno, man, looks like it just blew."

"No, someone definitely cut it." Drew pointed at a clean line at the rim. "Right there."

"Who'd do that?"

Don spat some blood, "I can guess."

"Man," Dale stood up. "You got a spare?"

"Yeah, but we'll have to push it off the berm first. You two lift the back and I'll drive it out."

"But the tire," Don protested.

Drew waved him off. "It'll be all right."

Took time, but they got it out, the Polara broadside in the middle of the dirt road. Stars wheeled and a crescent moon backlit the pines with a tad of silver, and the night rolled.

Don bent over catching his breath. "Stuck in the swamps of Jersey." He shook his head.

Stuck.

A rush of horror. "Hey!" Dale yelled, "Hey! What time is it, man?"

Drew was assembling the jack, the spare next to him. "You ain't gonna make it, bro."

"Oh nonononono, don't say shit like that, man, just don't say it."

"Sorry, but that's the truth."

"Look!" The fury was on him and he grabbed at the jack. "We gotta make it. Got to!"

"Hurry up, man. Hurry!"

Drew grabbed the jack back and shook it at him, "Look, dude, I know how to do this crap, you don't, and I'm telling you, we ain't gonna make it. So relax!"

Don straightened. "Besides, she ain't gonna be there, anyway."

Dale stepped back, speechless. Decision time.

He ran.

"Hey, what the, what the FUCK, man?" both of them calling, Don laughing, "You sure as hell ain't gonna make it on foot!"

He got to the turnoff for Springfield Road and

whirled. "Catch up to me, dudes!"

"What?" Drew yelled.

"Catch up to me! On the road. Catch up!" He turned but stopped because the moon moved the right way and they were spirits in the night, racing Don's Impala down this very road laughing and throwing beer at each other then drunk and stumbling, cold and shivering, from the beach to Don's house passing out on the basement floor and the Polka Hall in Groveville dancing with the local girls while Drew played and then running through the high school with the town girls and skipping to the Koffee Kup.

"Catch up to me," he pleaded. But they just stood there, silent, and he knew they wouldn't.

Ever.

A few cars passed back and forth and that's what he banked on and hit the asphalt hard, barely missing a pickup truck that blew its horn and swerved as someone yelled. He didn't care. He stepped into the middle of the road as headlights bore down. He was going to make it or die.

The car stopped. A head out the driver's window. A delighted voice. "Hey, man!"

Sonny.

Dale yanked the Camino's passenger door open. "Five dollars to get me to Gino's by midnight."

"Midnight?" Sonny shook his head. "No way, bro."

"Ten."

Sonny blinked. "Get in, strap in, and hang on."

Empty parking lot, the security lights from Gino's glowing the asphalt and glowing him, the most forlorn of objects, arms jammed into pockets, lost opportunity hammering him upside the head and laughing maniacally. Same old story: the bus pulling away as he made the stop, the movie selling out as he reached the booth, the door to the SATs closing as he ran down the hall. Dollar late, day short.

Fuck me.

Pop of gravel and crap underneath some tires coming up behind him. Great, probably cops or, worse, thugs. He readied for jail or war and missing the airport bus and subsequent warrants for AWOL or Desertion or whatever they charged guys who didn't have the stones to show up and that'd be fine, Mr. Sergeant Recruiter Man, So-Disappointed-in-You Son, because, well, his life was pretty much over, anyway.

A brown Coronet pulled up sideways. "You're late," she said out the driver's window.

"I know."

"What kept you?"

"Been a strange night."

"Hmm." She regarded him, "I can see that." She paused, sniffed. "Is that dope?"

"Yes."

"I don't do that."

"Okay."

"I don't drink, either."

"Okay."

"And …" sterner voice. He braced himself. "I don't … well, I will. Eventually. But not tonight." She waggled a finger at him. "I don't care if you're going to Vietnam."

"Vietnam's about over."

"I know, so that line won't work."

"Gotcha."

She grinned and there was just enough light from the topped moon to make her a tad silver and there was magic in the night.

"WOOOHOOO!" screamed from the road behind a pair of squealing tires and Dale watched Sonny's Camino fishtail down 38, fire and smoke coming off the road. "Goood luuuck brooo!" followed the fast-vanishing taillights.

"Friend of yours?" she asked.

"He is now."

She gestured to the passenger side. He walked around and slid onto the bench seat. He looked at her. The red slip of a uniform still held her jealously. "I thought you weren't going to wait."

"I changed my mind."

"Why?"

She regarded him. "Silly question."

He nodded. The radio was tuned to MMR. The

aurora rose behind him.

"What time's your bus?" she asked.

"8:00."

"Where?"

"Burlington."

She nodded. "You'll make it," and she turned her head and those eyes, amber and forever, lidded coquettishly at him. "And you'll definitely, definitely, want to come back."

They drove off.

From Darkness into Light

Thankful Tonight

Ed DeJesus

Historical Fiction |
Based on True Events

Tuesday, November 9, 1965, began like every school morning. But it sure ended differently for this fifteen-year-old boy in Lowell, Massachusetts, a mill town twenty-five miles northwest of Boston with a hundred thousand gritty residents.

I was fortunate to grow up in a ten-room, two-story tenement that my Dad, a WWII veteran, bought with a VA loan in 1950 and single-handedly converted to a single-family home. The steam radiators that clanged through asbestos-covered pipes, heated by a rumbling oil furnace in our dungy cellar, didn't always warm the drafty linoleum floors, but my three siblings and I had it good. My mornings started with the quick tempo of the Beatles bridge in "A Day In The Life,"

> *Woke up, fell out of bed, dragged a comb across my head…*
> *Found my coat and grabbed my hat, made the bus in seconds flat…*

But I never wore a hat or took the bus. Instead, I walked two extra miles before and after school for the job I held in my sophomore and junior years. I rushed out the back door at 6:50 a.m., my brisk pace necessary to make the 1.2-mile leg to my first stop by 7:10. It was chilly, and I had to be careful not to slip on the morning frost. I pulled my hood up and tucked my hands inside the pockets of my lined vinyl jacket—worn over my required school dress code, a burgundy V-neck sweater, button-down blue shirt, and paisley tie—it kept me warm and dry.

We lived in the city's deteriorated Lower Highlands, and I headed to the Upper Highlands. I rushed up Hale Street and reached the Abraham Lincoln Monument in the center of Lincoln Square. I dodged traffic and bolted across busy Chelmsford Street. I hiked up the steep Liberty Street hill, crossed Smith, Powell, and School streets, and turned right onto Hastings, which brought me to Cupples Square by Pages Drug Store on Westford Street.

The Timex on my wrist told me I had six minutes to reach my destination. I took a right down Dover Street to the intersection of Branch and Middlesex Street. I crossed to Middlesex, headed left, and walked briskly until I reached Wilder Street's corner. Then, I made my way up the driveway of my boss's home.

I checked my watch, cupped my ice-cold hands, and blew on them to keep them warm. At nine past seven, I rang the side doorbell of the stately two-family Victorian house. I heard the heavy footsteps of my hefty boss cautiously descending the back hallway stairs. "Good morning, Eddie," he cheerfully greeted me and locked the door from a key chain attached to his belt.

"Morning, George," I said, then hooked his left arm with my right arm and guided him down the porch steps and along the walkway to Wilder Street before steering him left onto Middlesex. I kept George on the inside, away from the street. Arm in arm and lockstep, we began our mile-long journey towards the downtown Lowell Workshop for the Blind on Middlesex Street.

George Zermas and seven other visually impaired coworkers made straw brooms and strung wicker chairs from 8:30 a.m. to 4:30 p.m. The modest-looking shop had a storefront window with a Lowell Association for the Blind sign and its touching tagline: ***From Darkness***

into Light.

Big, burly, jovial George was forty-two, nearly six feet, and weighed over two hundred pounds. I was only five-three then, but with strong legs and a stocky one-thirty-three frame, I had beaten everyone in my weight class. Coach Bossi wanted me on his wrestling team, but when I explained that I had an essential after-school job, he nodded and never asked again.

I'd never seen George use a white cane or seeing-eye dog like other blind people. He preferred conversation and companionship, so I was happy to oblige my Greek philosophical boss. He was therapeutic, letting me open up and talk about my family, friends, and relationships.

"How come so quiet today, Eddie?" George asked softly, tilting his head in my direction as we walked briskly. I replied, "I left my English book at home and have a test today."

"Oh good," he chuckled, poking me with his elbow. "I thought you were having trouble with your girlfriend, Suzy."

After dancing closely with Suzy Saturday night to rock bands at the Commodore Ballroom, things changed. I didn't want to share with George that the brief romance—between cute-as-a-button, too-shy Suzy and I—had faded quickly on our rendezvous in the cozy private seats in the rear of the Commodore. The sweet, innocent, French brunette from Pawtucketville with the turned-up nose and irresistibly perfect lips wasn't as receptive to making out as the more assertive girls I'd dated from the tougher neighborhoods and the housing projects.

Knowing George was a polished Tenor in a Lowell Barbershop Quartet, I asked him, "What songs did you sing Saturday?"

"Let Me Call You Sweetheart. And, of course, Shine on Harvest Moon," he said gleefully.

"Of course, it's that time of year," I said.

As one of my earliest mentors, I appreciated George's wisdom. Blind from birth—but with an enormous braille library in his second-floor apartment—he was intellectual. His sister Penelope lived on the first floor with her husband, Peter Demogenes. Penelope was Valedictorian at Lowell High, class of '38, and was a Professor Emerita at UMass Lowell, College of Education.

When we approached the School Street traffic light, I hit the button and held onto George until we could cross the street. Two doors down, I steered George around the broken beer bottle glass in front of the seedy tenement occupied by Lowell's Chapter of Hell's Angels. George wrinkled his nose as we both stifled the rancid scents of the overflowing trash cans. A row of Harley-Davidson Choppers were lined up like dominoes in the driveway. We moved on quickly.

George and I were near Washington Park on Middlesex Street when we heard the beep of the bread route driver, who slowed and offered us a ride. It never mattered how cold it was; I watched the vapor come out of his mouth as he routinely declined. The city bus loaded with my Lowell High classmates from the upper highlands passed by; I kept my head down under my hood and pretended I didn't see them gawking at us. It wouldn't happen today; no kids would look up from their phones.

The most challenging part of our journey was getting George safely across the hectic rotary and dual intersections known as the Lord Overpass, which spanned Thorndike Street. For anyone outside New England, a rotary was a roundabout, only crazier, especially when it had a main street below with eight off-and-on ramps.

There were no traffic lights then. I gripped George's arm tighter while we hurried across the rotary and descended the ramp on Middlesex Street. We passed by the Registry of Motor Vehicles building, and two doors beyond the Workshop for The Blind, we entered Picanso's Café, where George had breakfast every morning. In addition to my modest one-dollar-a-day pay, George would also buy me a cup of coffee and an English muffin, totaling a quarter back then.

I got George settled in a booth; the owner, Arthur Picanso, asked George how he wanted his eggs today. I'd finished my muffin and was sipping coffee. George was still working on his scrambled eggs and sausage links. He reminded me, "Tonight is Dicky Doyle's surprise birthday party. Be here at five-fifteen." Dick, the oldest blind man at the workshop, was turning sixty. Instead of getting George by 4:30 when the shop closed, I'd come to Picanso's.

George pulled out his leather wallet and unzipped it to pay the check. It had a change pocket that snapped shut, and he knew every coin's value by its size. In his billfold, the singles were kept flat, the fives folded in half, the tens folded in half length-wise, and the rare twenties were folded in thirds. He never accepted deuces or large bills. His sister would drive him to work if I were sick. Except for snow days, I had perfect attendance. Aside from two weeks in July when the workshop was closed, I was George's weekday guide for the other fifty.

George sipped his bottomless cup, and other visually impaired gentlemen arrived for coffee along with Leo, the shop's foreman. George would be in good hands as I headed to school. Instead of taking the bus route where all the shops and business fronts were on Middlesex to Central to Merrimack Street, I took the shortcut through the alley to the Jackson Street mills.

I crossed Jackson, took the driveway over the Hamilton bridge, and caught a nasty whiff of whatever the mills were discharging into the black, murky canal water. I hustled across the parking lot to the red brick Market Street building that today houses Lowell's National Historical Park Museum, which features the amazing industrial history of America's first planned city.

In the early 1800s, it was built along the Merrimack River to provide hydropower for the cotton mills' loom presses. Irish, Greek, English, and German immigrants hand-dug nearly six miles of canals to connect to the Concord and Charles Rivers to transport manufactured goods to Boston Harbor and nationwide railways. The mill owners built row houses for their employees and boarded its mill girls, who came from farms to earn a living, with as many as six to a room.

Lowell became a magnate for entrepreneurs, capital, worldwide labor, and talent. It was essentially the Silicon Valley of 19th-century America. The city grew rapidly, and by 1865, its fifty-two mills were turning 800,000 pounds of cotton into 2.4 million yards of cloth each week. Blankets were manufactured for the military for every world war. However, by the 1970s, many of the mills had closed, and unemployment was higher than in any city in America. [i]

I crossed Merrimack Street and entered Lowell High School by the Kirk Street Clock—just in time to get to my locker and first bell. School got out at 2:15 p.m. My close classmates and I hung out in front of the Dutch Tea Room restaurant on Merrimack Street. Most students waited across the street in front of the Bon Marché department store, where the city's buses were. They would transport them to Lowell's distinct ethnic (French-Canadian, Irish, Greek-German, and Portuguese neighborhoods): the Acre, Belvidere, Centralville, the Grove, Highlands, Pawtucketville, Sacred Heart, and South Lowell.

Several popular girls gathered on the sidewalk, clutching their schoolbooks, waiting for their buses to arrive. A handsome driver pulled to the curb in a sharp '57 Chevy Bel Air with the windows down and radio blaring. An attractive senior with long black hair and shapely legs in a plaid miniskirt approached the car. She slid in the coupe and waved goodbye to her giddy friends while McCartney's voice poured out onto Merrimack Street, *"Oh, I Believe in Yesterday."*

After the busses departed and the crowds thinned, I climbed the stairs to Alex's billiards room to shoot pool, as I did every day for over a year, biding time before I picked up George. I played snooker for an hour to sharpen my eye for future nine-ball games at fifty cents per money ball. I observed a preppy college guy take forever to beat another inexperienced player and knew I had my mark. He broke and left the table wide open. A few shots later, I sunk the five-ball, made an extra money ball, ran the rest of the table, and collected my winnings.

I left the pool hall forty minutes later than usual to get George. It was already dusk when I entered Picanso's café and found George and his boisterous co-workers crowded in a booth. Remnants of burgers, fries, coffee, and birthday cake littered the table and tiled floor. A bottle of Jameson and shot glasses were in front of Dick

Doyle, the birthday boy; his guide, Bobby Gervais, sat next to him; Leo, the workshop foreman, and George sat across from them.

Leo handed me a napkin and a piece of chocolate cake. I thanked him and George shouted, "Eddie!" when he heard my voice. I wished Dick a happy birthday and devoured the cake. I used a napkin to wipe frosting off George's chin, brushed crumbs from the front of his jacket, and bid goodnight to the party animals.

It was dark and chilly when we stepped onto Middlesex Street at 5:25. We walked arm and arm past the old Registry, RMV building. When we reached the Middlesex street ramp, all the lamp posts lighting the sidewalks went out. *Lord, help us.* It was pitch-dark as we ascended the ramp towards the Lord Overpass! Horns honked incessantly as we reached the top of the busy rotary. I looked to my left, and no lights were shining on the Commodore's marquee billboard, and to my right, I could not see the Wilder Grain buildings by the canal. No lights were on in any of the homes ahead in the highlands, nor the stores we left behind us.

I froze at the curb, hesitant to cross the first busy intersection. I pulled George tighter and tried to stop my trembling. The headlights from oncoming cars blinded me, and the panicked, hectic rush-hour drivers struggled to adjust to the darkness. "What's going on, Eddie?" George asked, a scent of whiskey on his breath.

"I don't know. All the city lights are out. It's pitch

dark, and we must move quickly across the rotary. Hang on tight and keep up." "Okay," he shouted over the blaring horns.

I raised my free hand to stop the traffic and hustled George to the other side of the first intersection. I rushed us along, and while the horns kept honking, we repeated the process on the second section of the rotary. When we descended the ramp on the other side of Middlesex Street, I slowed down, took a deep breath, and said, "Whew, I've never seen anything like this."

"It looks the same to me, ha-ha," George said, nudging my side to calm my nerves.

Today, George's cliché might have been, "Welcome to my world." And at that moment, I had a partial sense of what it was like for George to navigate in his world.

Candles illuminated windows on many of the triple-decker and multifamily homes we walked by on Middlesex Street. Residents sat on their front steps with cigarette lighters firing their tobacco sticks. As we approached the busy School Street traffic light that wasn't working, a loud, deafening roar of two motorcycle engines started up in a driveway and blinded me with their headlights. I stopped abruptly and felt George's arm tighten. The Hell's Angels revved their Harley Choppers, pulled out, and roared up Middlesex Street.

When my heart stopped racing, I picked up our pace and continued down Middlesex Street until we reached the corner of Wilder. As we approached, I saw the shadow of someone holding a flashlight and aiming it at our feet.

"Thank God, you made it!" George's sister Penelope said as she touched his shoulder and patted my arm. She explained what she'd heard on her car radio: "The power is out in Massachusetts and several other northeast states."

Silhouettes lingered by windows illuminated with flickering candles while I jogged home through the eerily dark side streets and sprinted across the horn-blowing main streets. My dad's '58 Pontiac Bonneville was parked in the driveway. The former Army Medic had made it home safely from his job at the Veteran's Administration hospital in Bedford, Mass.

I entered the back door. My older sister was doing her homework on the kitchen counter by candlelight. My mom turned away from the gas stove and hugged me. Dad and my big brother in the parlor listened to the news of the northeast blackout on a transistor radio. My younger brother shined a flashlight on me and shouted, "Teddy's home! Let's eat. I'm starving."

We gathered at our candle-lit dining room table. It wasn't a feast like Thanksgiving—but before our close-knit catholic family enjoyed chicken pot pie, mashed potatoes, and biscuits—we said grace and were thankful tonight. I told them about my adventure with my boss. Mom made a sign of the cross, my big brother high-fived me, my sister and kid brother smiled, and I sensed my

Dad was proud of me for getting George home safely.

Years later, I toiled in technology but kept in touch with George 'til he passed. His late sister, Penelope Z. Demogenes, set up a memorial grant for George. Each year, the Lowell Association for the Blind held a competition for the George E. Zermas Memorial Scholarships for worthy students preparing to work with the blind and visually impaired. [ii]

The old workshop with wicker chairs is long gone, and it has been moved to a large high-tech facility with braille computer keyboards and audio aids. The Lowell Association for the Blind, established in 1923, continues to support visually impaired people, and they still have the same tagline: ***From Darkness into Light***. [iii]

Senior citizens may recall where they were when thirty million people in ten states and parts of Canada lost power in the 1965 blackout. Initially, it was rumored to be a Russian terrorist attack as we were in a cold war with them and losing troops in Vietnam. But that was deemed false, along with the rumor that we had a baby boom nine months later. [iiii]

I know how disruptive power outages are, as I retired in Florida and survived several category-four hurricanes and a recent heart attack. Consequently, I don't need turkey, pumpkin pie, and football games to remind me of what I'm thankful for.

Lastly, I always get homesick and moved by the Bee Gees' ballad, "Massachusetts."

Feel I'm goin' back to Massachusetts.
Something's telling me I must go home.
And the lights all went out in Massachusetts...
And Massachusetts is one place I have seen

Enjoy: The Bee Gees - Massachusetts (1967) - YouTube

[I] Source: *Legendary Locals of Lowell*, Richard P. Howe Jr. and Chaim M. Rosenberg 2013.
[ii] Source: (1) Facebook
[iii] Source: Lowell Association for the Blind.org Home | LAB
[iiii] Source: Northeast blackout of 1965 - Wikipedia

The Outside Clan

Lisa Towles

Historical Fiction

1958

My sisters Shelby and Cleo came with me the day I got lost in the woods. It had rained for three consecutive weeks; everything gray, everything the same. As we scattered rampant over the pulpy ground and through leafy knobs of sycamore, the sky started to break up. Our fleeing shadows, beneath a barely visible, fuzzy moon, resembled naked souls in a state of unrest. I hurried, like this, through my entire childhood. By the time I left home, each day seemed cloaked by a routine state of panic.

The summer I turned eight, Cleo and I burned down

the living room. It started out as nothing at all; an accident, a spark, really, from a modest heap of Mama's cigarette droppings. Despite her acrimonious threats, we'd been smoking again on the windowsill behind the living room curtains. From the beginning, Mama blamed me for being a bad influence on Cleo, two years younger. By peeking through the spokes in the railing, Cleo and I used to watch Mama suck down unfiltered Pall Malls one after the other. Something innately sexual about how she did it intrigued us. She understood things about the power of her own beauty. While leaning against the kitchen table, she arched her head back with her chest out and elbows on the tablecloth. We never knew who she was showing off to. "Maybe she's practicing," I suggested.

"For what?" Cleo asked, unprepared for the answer.

We'd creep up to our room after and pretend to smoke Ticonderoga pencils. Then one day we tried it for real.

In the tiniest fraction of time, flames lunged from the tops of the curtains to the ceiling and then down again to the china cabinet. As a collective reflex, Cleo and I dropped down onto the shag carpet and lay on our stomachs with our hands over our hair. Oh God, don't let me die, I said to myself. I haven't been kissed yet. Not more than ten seconds later, the room was filled with smoke and our bodies were blocks of lead. In lumbering pulls, I tried my best to drag Cleo behind me through the dense fumes. But time reduced itself to half speed and gravity had doubled. Each step left me trembling with terror and exhaustion.

"Mama," I wailed as loud as I could. "Mama!!!" But she wasn't listening for my voice, that day or any day.

And by the time I reached the back porch, I discovered I was alone.

Our older sister Shelby tried to help. She was ten that year, at a time in my life when thirteen seemed as old as one could get. Much taller than all the other girls her age, Shelby stood on the coffee table, yanked the curtains off the rod and began stomping out flames with her new birthday boots. Shelby possessed courage like Hercules had strength. I'll never forget the steely look on her face as she dragged Cleo's limp body through the foggy living room. That was supposed to be my job. I cried when they reached the back porch.

Cleo looked shrunken in her long hospital bed, like the size of her Penny doll. She was shrouded in a wash of white curtains, white sheets, and nurses in white smocks and shoes. Sickness burrowed through her tiny body like microscopic moles, and for two weeks we thought she might die. Mama refused to look at me in the hospital waiting room. While the doctor relayed to us the miserable condition of Cleo's lungs, Mama could scarcely breathe. Cleo had always been her favorite. We all knew. Three weeks later Belle, the friendly nurse, put Cleo in a wheelchair and took her for a spin around the fifth floor.

By suppertime that night, she'd contracted viral pneumonia. She didn't leave the hospital for three months.

Mama smoked her last cigarette on Christmas morning. I could tell it was her last one because she closed her eyes to inhale and wept as the final streams of smoke left her lips. In her heart, I think Cleo was still her favorite, but something had changed, for all of us. The dynamic of our self-contained, nuclear family seemed irrevocably altered. After a brutal recovery, Cleo still limped when she walked, and over-exertion left her pale and wheezing. So sometime in the latter part of 1962, Shelby became Mama's surrogate favorite. For Christmas gifts that year, Cleo and I got hand-loomed rugs made out of spun, dyed sheep's wool from a Shoshone woman Mama met at a quilting bee. Shelby got a brand new violin.

"But I don't want to play the violin," Shelby screamed infant-like beneath the yellow slaps of my mother's palm. In the years I'd been her sister, not once had I seen her cry. Mama's attention meant nothing to Shelby. To Cleo and me, it meant enough air to breathe.

Onions grew in our beet patch the next spring. We hadn't planted bulbs and no one knew where they came from. Mama called it the divine harvest. All at once, we seemed to have things we'd needed for so long. New shoes, a new metal trough for the horses, someone to repair the barn doors and broken furnace. The mysterious bounty of vegetables put us all in the most peculiar, smiling trance. Cleo cleaned under her bed; I did chores without being asked. One time, a man we didn't know came to visit Mama and brought a bouquet of pink flowers. They all disappeared into her bedroom and the man was gone before breakfast.

1963

Mama sold the farm in November and moved us into a house closer to civilization. The farming got to be too much after Daddy died. Cleo and I liked the big house in town. We discovered hidden rooms and cedar closets, and the small barn in back had a split-door where you could open just the top. Shelby, fourteen by now and a grown-up in our minds, used to take boys into the hay loft and let them touch her anywhere for a dollar. With her discovery of the swelling mounds on her chest, Shelby's new walk evoked attention like she were running stark naked through the streets. I watched people notice her -- ranchers, their sons and grandsons. The women mostly looked away. At night she modeled Mama's brassieres for Cleo and me, and demonstrated the application of lipstick. After an examination of my own smooth, flat chest, I was sure I had to be a boy. I could discern no other explanation for my lack of breasts and pubic hair. I'll never grow up, I remember thinking.

So in the interest of learning about girlhood, I devised a plan to spy on Shelby by climbing up to the loft before she got there. After just one time, Cleo got sick again and was too cumbersome to carry up the steep loft steps.

We had spectacular neighbors surrounding that house. Mama called them vagrant out-of-work hillbillies. Yolanda lived behind us on top of a grassy slope. A husbandless, middle-aged woman who wore expensive clothes, women came to her house late at night and they listened to jazz on the radio and danced in their living room. Shelby told me she was a lesbian call girl. I had no idea what this meant, but I knew it must be exotic. An Asian man with a collection of antique swords above his fireplace lived to the left of us in the small house with no front door. He meditated a lot and seemed so ethereal in his movements. I used to imagine he entered the dwelling by passing through walls. A Lebanese family moved into the house on the other side with the ghost in the basement. We could smell their curious food through the screen door on hot summer nights. Lamb, mint, hearty grains. Arayah, the girl my age, taught me some Arabic phrases. The words, when she spoke them, sounded so beautiful, elegant almost. I was just a hick and didn't have the correct muscle movements to fit properly around the exotic sounds.

Marcus

Shortly after moving, Mama took a job at a quilt store

in Cody. Cleo needed constant care and it was the only way to pay for an in-house doctor. I accidentally ran into him on his first day. The collision knocked the wind out of me.

"You must be Charmaine, Cleo's sister. I'm Dr. Vanderloo. But you may call me Marcus," he commanded and whisked me up into his arms like a half-filled sack of potatoes. "You're going to be all right," he said in response to my gasping and coughing.

Dr. Vanderloo's presence created turmoil in our house at first. Without proper notification, he took the liberty of bringing along his wife and an Australian Blue Heeler named Popo. Popo turned out to be one of those crotch-sniffing, friendly dogs. Mama threatened to kill it every time Marcus turned his back. Marcus introduced his wife as Geneva, but I knew he called her Jeannie in the privacy of their bedroom. During their first week's stay, Cleo and I listened with a glass cup against the bathroom wall every night. Geneva bathed after breakfast every morning, though I could never understand how someone could get dirty just from sleeping. And a collection of European perfumes stood like shiny glass soldiers on her walnut vanity table. We were poor. We were not like her. Not in the least. To Cleo and me, Geneva was a goddess, with her lion-mane of golden hair wrapped neatly under itself on top of her head. We watched her braid it once in the time it takes to sneeze. She spoke without barely moving her mouth and called us "Kittens."

In order to procure free room and board, the Vanderloos made themselves useful around the house. I caught Marcus, once, shirtless and wiping his brow, perched high on some rented scaffolding used to repair the ceiling. So graphic and raw was his hairy armpit marbled with bulging muscles and the glistening, oily sweat on his skin. Peering at him from behind the kitchen wall, my face got so hot I thought I might faint. That was the first sensation I ever remember feeling in my groin. At that moment, I knew I was not destined to be small and awkward forever. All three of us girls fell in love with Marcus, but I had it the worst. Against Geneva's stark features and resolute blondeness, I felt dark and shriveled like a dying Gypsy child. I hated her for this. I wanted to cry every time Marcus kissed her. For him, I would have cut off my leg and let myself bleed to death.

From the neighbors we learned that Doctor Vanderloo had married into money. They maintained a small house on a Greek island in the Aegean Sea. Geneva told us about it many times. We sat on the front porch, all of us, drinking hot cider out of jelly jars. Mama put a cinnamon stick in the side of each jar, and the grownups got theirs spiked with rum. Cleo had just returned from the hospital again and was wearing a new woolen suit Marcus bought her. She'd lost almost twenty pounds this time; her clothes seemed knotted up around her, half tucked in, misbuttoned. She looked like the scarecrow we put up in the backyard. I wanted to cry every time I looked at her. Geneva seemed to understand this and put her long white hand on my shoulder.

"My ancestors have always lived in Aegina, although I was born in New York and have never even been to Greece," she said twirling a fallen strand of hair.

We all stayed quiet, clinging to her thoughts and words while she reverted into some forgotten trance. The air outside on the porch chilled our cider even before the first sip, but no one moved.

"Somewhere in my mind, I live in Aegina. Not necessarily with Marcus, but very close by. My hair is cropped short like a boy's, and I wear long, dangly earrings and very little makeup. My complexion is buffed to a flawless glow from the winds on the beach every day. I jog across white sands at dawn and drink fresh-squeezed juices. During the day, I write children's stories and create charcoal drawings to hang on my slab walls.

"My house is a single-story stucco hut painted white, with arched doorways and alcove ceilings, and round rugs hand-braided by local merchants. Every night, supper of shaved lamb, Retsina and souvlaki with the year-rounders is followed by square dancing. The music comes from the twang of ancient dulcimers and the sounding bliss of the emerald sea polishing the shore."

So absorbed by this imagery, I swore I could hear

seagulls and smell low tide. The potent amalgam of Geneva's words and grainy voice somehow transformed our small-town world into something entirely cosmopolitan. After that night, Shelby began buying fashion magazines and cutting out pictures of leggy models to hang on her walls. She eventually adapted her own personal style to this shallow ideal, changing her wardrobe of mostly overalls to sleek, black clothing and tall boots.

Posse

With Daddy gone, Marcus and Geneva stayed on long after Cleo got well. Mama never asked them or addressed the matter directly; they knew she needed someone to look after us and she tolerated their constant presence. Shelby, by this time, had developed a nasty habit of staying out late and sometimes not returning for days. Mama, who called this routine "prowling," always went looking for her and didn't come home until she found her. Cleo and I knew where Shelby went every night, yet this information remained privileged and sacred. Bubba Savage lived on the other side of Cody, the Yellowstone side. We lived on the side facing Powell. Bubba drove a motorcycle and was old enough to buy beer. When he courted Shelby, Bubba parked his bike on Happy Jack Road two miles away and hiked through the woods to the big rock on the far edge of our property. Marcus knew Shelby was in trouble, and he knew he could count on me for anything. From the start, my lack of self-control around him infuriated me. I watched Shelby in the company of men. She knew how to be coy, how to flirt with her eyes and make them do whatever she wanted, but she could turn it off in a single blink. Where did she learn such a foreign skill, I often asked myself. Daddy died when I was six. I had no idea how to act around men.

"Charmaine, come over here," Marcus said with a daring smile -- straight, white teeth framed by red lips and a darkly graying mustache. I considered his green eyes part of his smile. They somehow personalized what would otherwise be a distant, rugged face. Oh God, I thought. There was nothing I wouldn't tell him now. Cleo sent me telepathic threats from across the room, hip to Marcus's power over me. He picked me up and sat me on his lap, a gesture I'd clearly outgrown. He angled his lips close to my ear and spoke in a feather voice.

"My dear, we are all very worried about your sister," he said. I saw Geneva in the kitchen trying not to listen. Mama did the same by wiping already-dried dishes. "Would you tell me where you think she is?" he asked with a glare so intense and penetrating I had to look down at my dress to be sure I wasn't naked. This possibility endured for several seconds before my resolve caved in.

"She's gone to Bubba's cabin on the Mackland's

ranch," I mechanically replied. While Cleo scalded me with her eyes, Marcus rewarded this capital betrayal with a kiss on my cheek and a long squeeze. I felt his heart beating through his shirt. Well worth the consequences, I thought.

The grownups left together in a sort of search posse. With everyone else gone, Cleo and I crept upstairs to Mama's bedroom. In and of itself, this act would not go unpunished. But she had the only electric blanket in the house and the heat was turned off. Oddly, we both noticed the distinct odor of tobacco on Mama's sheets. We knew she had quit long before, yet we found a curiously soiled ashtray on the nightstand beside her bed. Cleo pulled the power button on Mama's black and white television. At first we didn't notice what program was showing, as it would have interrupted our scavenger hunt through Mama's jewelry box and underwear drawers. Cleo found a foiled package of yellow pills, and I found what I thought was the oddest garment I'd ever seen.

"It's a garter," Cleo said. Cleo, my younger sister, knew this.

"How would you know?" I demanded.

She thought for a moment. "Shelby has one. She showed me how to put it on."

I asked Cleo what she looked like in it, but she wasn't listening. Her eyes had gotten stuck on the television screen. My eyes followed hers and soon became glued to the moving images. At the same moment, our breathing stopped and our jaws hung open. Neither of us moved. As I watched the sultry woman, dark skinned and naked except for the bath towel around her head, I thought of Marcus. How would he look at me if I were grown up and looked like that? After requisite kissing, the man placed the woman gently on the unmade bed and lay down on her, groping her private places. While his hand reached down between her legs, the woman remained smiling, laughing almost. How could this be? Marcus, I kept thinking. What if he did those vile things to Geneva? What if he undressed her and got up on top of her all sweaty everywhere like the man on the television? Was Marcus like that man? Was Geneva that kind of woman? When I saw Cleo bite down on her bottom lip, I turned off the television.

I made dinner for two out of peanut butter and jelly sandwiches and chicken soup out of a can. Cleo ate in silence; I made contrived efforts at conversation by rehashing old bits of gossip.

"Did you hear about the Sugar Beet Festival?"

"No," she replied.

"They canceled it on account of the crop damage from all that rain. The Iverson's didn't get a quarter the harvest they got last year."

But Cleo's eyes looked lost in the trauma of our broken childhood.

By the time the grownups returned, it had been dark

for hours. Shelby walked in first with torn pants and mud streaked across her cheeks.

"What have you been doing?" I asked her, but the Shelby I knew was not there. In her face I saw someone, or something, altogether unfamiliar. No one said much for the rest of the night. Mama and Geneva disappeared with Shelby, who had to be shoved up the stairs screaming. Over the next several hours, Marcus sat in his rocking chair flipping through medical textbooks, and Cleo and I tried to fall asleep despite the noises coming from Shelby's room upstairs. The first time I heard it, I felt my heart in my throat.

"What was that?" Cleo asked, running to the edge of my bed. I held her hand with a reassurance I couldn't even give myself.

"I don't know. Something happened to Shelby, I think."

Cleo drew her hand to her mouth. "She's crying. What's going on in there? I want to go see."

"No!" I hissed, restraining her against the side of my bed. "Mama and Geneva are there. She'll be alright." This was a lie, though. I'd never been so scared my whole life. What began in Shelby's room as a flutter of quiet sobs quickly turned into uncontrollable shrieking. All of my thirty-something feet of intestines contracted into the size of a baseball. Cleo is younger, I kept reminding myself. I must remain composed.

Early the next morning, I watched the sun make its

slow ascent over the pink mountains in the distance. Lying on my back facing the window, I tried to remember a saying from my childhood, "Red sky at morning, sailors take warning. Red sky at night, sailors delight..." I heard Mama put water on for coffee shortly after I woke. This, I decided, was an opportunity in disguise. Without saying a word, I crept up to the kitchen table and watched her nervous, choppy movements. By the way her back moved, I could sense her erratic breathing. From the time Daddy died in the barn seven years ago, she hadn't looked right. Looking at a back view of her now -- hips narrow and contracted, hair dry and feet pointed in, I knew pain had gnawed away at her most vital traits. I couldn't tell if she sensed my presence or not. When she turned around and noticed me, we both seemed to gasp at the same time. In that moment, I relived the waiting room scene in the hospital when Cleo's lungs got burned in the fire. This is what Mama's face looked like now. Eyes bloodshot, creased and folded in, pallid complexion, mouth vexed and compressed into a tiny pink dot.

"I didn't know you were here," she said and turned away.

"Mama, I want to know about Shelby."

Her movements froze at the toaster. Bread stuck in her left hand, butter knife stuck in her right, she stared at the wall. And as elegantly as Ginger Rogers danced in her long white dress in the movie "Top Hat," Mama reached her gnarled hand into the top drawer and withdrew a leather case. I watched her welcome a cigarette to her lips like an old friend.

"Do you know what the word 'defiled' means, Charmaine?"

She looked haunted. I was afraid to answer. For some reason, I crossed my legs.

"It means Bubba Savage took something from your sister he shouldn't have."

I glanced out the window, just as a reprieve from the tension. The ceiling of low, dark clouds made the world a dark, enclosed place. "Can Shelby get it back?" I asked, realizing too late how stupid it sounded.

Mama tried not to laugh. Instead, she dragged deeply on the cigarette. I waited, but no answer came. I heard Marcus moving around upstairs; I recognized the weight of his footsteps against the hardwood floors. Geneva turned on the water faucet to run her morning bath. Things were happening; people were waking up. I needed answers now because I knew none would be available after today. This incident, like the living room fire, would soon become one of those things people only discuss with their eyes. From the rear of my brain, I heard Marcus open the front door and go outside. Mama glared at me, her weary eyes blinking.

"I heard a story one time of some of our ancestors from way back who had a little stone house in the center of a plantation."

"Where?" I asked.

"Down south near Laramie," she said.

"What kind of plantation?"

"I don't know. I think beans and alfalfa mostly. But they used this little stone house for cooking. Just for cooking," she repeated to enhance the delivery, like she was searching for something in my face.

"These people cooked inside, but slept outside every night in the back of the barn. Not even a barn, really. More like a lean-to because it had no ceiling. There was a dirt floor and a detached side wall where they hung their overcoats, boots and farming tools."

Why was she telling me this, I wondered on the verge of tears. I wanted to know about Shelby. "What does this have to do with Shelby?" I insisted.

Mama cried now, and let the tears fall into her ashtray. "That's where I found her," she weeped. "I found her in a place just like that. A little hut with no ceiling, no clothes on her, one of her legs lying in the dirt, blood on her bruised face." Nothing was said for a long time after that. Marcus came back in the house and put his strong arms around Mama. I thought, then, of all the men I had known. I thought of Daddy, of Bubba, and then I looked up at Marcus. He put his arms around me without lifting a finger.

Aegina

Seventeen years later, I found my legs dangling off

the edge of a ferry en route to Aegina. After two children and just as many marriages, my physique surprised most people. I remember Shelby telling me once that I would always have strong legs from walking to school every day. A man sitting across from me had been staring at my lower half for most of the trip. My own fault, really, since I'd chosen shorts and a tank top as the day's attire.

"I'm Gabriel," the man said with a smile that revealed glorious white teeth.

This smile seemed the least of what was familiar to me now. Marcus had encompassed my every thought since departing the aircraft in Athens. Gabriel and I were alone on the lower level, so obviously we would get to know each other. I groaned at his presence, though, and politely looked away to return to the ghosts of my past.

"Do you have friends in Aegina?" he asked me, and why did he care? Did I look like I didn't belong there? I had to think for a moment. His English was choppy but he obviously knew the words.

"I used to."

"Where do they live now?"

"Well," I tried to explain, "they lived with us when I was very young. The woman's family lived in Aegina." I shrugged. "That's all I know."

Gabriel smiled at my words. "You are a brave woman traveling all this way on hope."

"Yes," I laughed. "Hope."

Our small ferry had taken on rainwater earlier, which

drained through the portholes in the side. The promise of another storm filled the sky and atmosphere. Communication screeched to a halt when the winds began. The boat weaved clumsily through the forest of crested waves. Gabriel moved to my side of the boat at the request of the crew, a command I could tell he didn't mind following. Near him, I felt small again like I had around Marcus. And oddly safe.

"What are the names of your friends?" he asked, almost yelling now in response to a sudden rain.

I stared at his face, searching for something I couldn't explain. "Dr. Marcus Vanderloo. His wife was —"

Almost as if Gabriel heard my words before they even left my mouth, his smile interrupted my train of thought.

"Geneva. It was a long time ago."

"They have four children," he said. "The eldest is Marcus, Jr. We work together on a fishing boat."

While my mouth hung open a few inches, no thoughts came to mind. Could this be possible? Was Marcus here, and did this man really know him? "Are you certain?" I managed to ask, nearly crying. Gabriel grabbed my hand and held it until we reached port.

The Vanderloo home stood strong on the edge of a rocky hill, like it had in so many of my dreams. From the road, Marcus was a spec of a man looking in my direction. But as I neared him, his grand stature rose like a giant against the emerald Aegean. Gabriel kept his arm around my back as some lame gesture of ownership. I made my hand unavailable to him by clutching one of my bags. The sun began to set an hour before, and now its shadows decorated the sky like the frosting on birthday cakes.

As we approached the house, Gabriel said, "You know, I've always thought that love hurts the most when you pretend not to feel it."

While I knew these words had been handpicked for the present occasion, I had other priorities. Marcus, ten feet away now, began running toward me. He had tears in his eyes.

"I knew you would come," he laughed. His embrace raised me up off the ground. We were almost dancing. "After all these years, I always knew."

Right away, I learned that Geneva died three years before of heart complications. Out of some solidarity, Gabriel had neglected to tell me this on the ferry. "She was never strong like you girls," Marcus said with a paternal air. Could it be that he thought of me, Cleo and Shelby as his surrogate daughters? I hated this idea. I hated how Marcus kissed me on the forehead when he saw me.

"What about your family?" he asked after storing my luggage in a spare bedroom.

Mama, like Geneva, died of a heart attack when she was forty-five. I told him about how Cleo went to college and worked as an insurance broker on the East Coast. "And Shelby," I started, which brought an instant smile to his face, "teaches riding lessons to children on her cattle ranch in Casper."

The day after my arrival, I met Marcus's family of three handsome sons and a pregnant daughter. His two oldest boys took me out sponge-fishing which I learned was, besides tourism, Aegina's main industry. His daughter, Tara, had suspicions about me from the start. At our first meeting, she squeezed my hand like an empty tube of toothpaste.

"We are twenty years apart in age," Marcus said one night after dinner, attempting to address what had lingered unresolved for so long. "You have blossomed just like I pictured. But after all this time being away, I cannot define what is between us."

Though the question remained unanswered, Marcus and I sat up all night on his balcony overlooking the water, listening to the waves, and seagulls, and watching our thoughts wash out to sea.

Blood at the Window

• • ● • •

Timothy Baldwin

Psychological Thriller

Beneath the fluorescent lights of Aspire Financial Network, Dwayne Church taps with rhythm and precision on his keyboard. He's been this way for days, a calm and efficient presence inspiring his team to excel at opening new accounts.

As his call ends, Dwayne glances at the leaderboard and smiles. Over the last week, his name rose in ranks on the company leaderboard. Now, his team holds second place for approved credit card applications. One more team to take out before he reaches the top. Though his smile fades when he sees whose team he has to beat— Sarah Anderson.

As if on cue, he logs off his computer and rises. Turning to a team member, he says with a wink, "Open two more accounts for me."

The middle-aged woman punches a key, prompting a window to open up as she follows a scripted conversation with someone on the other end of the line.

Dwayne frowns and turns away. The woman didn't give him so much as a nod at his attempt at team camaraderie.

Why should I care about her? Or them? Dwayne thinks as he passes the countless nameless faces of Aspire's employees. *In no time, I'll surpass them all. Then Sarah and I will celebrate with a night out.*

With the makings of his master plan taking shape, Dwayne passes through the first security checkpoint. A few coworkers wave at him. He raises his head high and takes the stairs down to the second floor, bypassing the fat, lazy individuals who choose the escalator, or worse, the elevator, every day.

But not Sarah.

Like him, she incorporates micro fitness sessions daily and hits the gym hard around lunch time. One perk of Aspire, aside from the company gym, is the flexible hours. So long as employees meet their weekly goals, they can do whatever they want. Some choose long lunches at the chain restaurant serving burgers and fries. But not Dwayne. He opts to log hours at the gym and chase his workouts with a salad and a protein shake.

Just as he's seen Sarah do hundreds of times.

In the locker room, Dwayne wastes no time bullshitting with the guys. Instead, he changes out of his suit and tie, neatly hanging them in his assigned locker. Slipping on his Under Armour gear, he catches his reflection in the mirror. His broad shoulders and expanded chest and biceps contrast with the wiry frame of his former self, a testament to his dedication and hard work.

Hard work in the gym and on the sales floor makes for a successful man.

Stepping out of the locker room, Dwayne scans the gym floor. A handful of men and women use the free weights. But most run at varying paces on the treadmills —rabbits in a race to nowhere, just like their failed attempts to meet the ever-increasing demand for more accounts.

But not Sarah.

Dwayne passes the elliptical trainers and rowers. He doesn't so much as glance at the universal machines. However, Dwayne can't help but grin upon seeing Sarah at the Smith machine, honing her glutes while doing pelvic thrusts. Yet it's not at this he grins, nor at the spandex she wears, which leaves little room for the imagination. Instead, he sees the open machine next to Sarah, allowing him a perfect opportunity for casual conversation.

While Sarah continues her set, Dwayne adjusts the

bench and barbell at his station. Upon racking the weights, he glances at Sarah. She looks straight ahead while her chest rises and falls with each deep breath.

"Hey," Dwayne says, stretching out his triceps. Dwayne's face flushes when he realizes Sarah is wearing noise-canceling earbuds. On his next stretch, he repositions himself into her line of sight and waves.

Sarah makes eye contact with Dwayne and removes an earbud. "Sorry," she says. "Did you say something?"

At a momentary loss for words, Dwayne fumbles. "Yeah… just saying 'hey.'"

"Cool," Sarah says and replaces her earbuds.

"How about drinks tonight?" Dwayne asks.

"I thought I made myself clear the last time, Dwayne. I come here to work out, not be picked up by male coworkers who think they are God's gift to women."

"I don't think—"

"If you'll excuse me," Sarah says. "I have two more sets before I switch machines."

Sarah refocuses her attention forward. Dwayne shifts his gaze away from her sculpted abs, beading with sweat.

Plopping onto the bench, Dwayne slaps the barbell once, then lies on his back. Lifting the barbell and lowering it to his chest, he attempts to throw himself into the first set. But as he counts, his mind is on Sarah, the profoundly beautiful and determined woman beside him who might as well be miles away.

Gritting his teeth, Dwayne struggles to swallow back

his embarrassment, only for it to turn to anger as he pushes the barbell for an eighth rep. By his twelfth rep, he fumes.

He's taken it slow with Sarah, attempted to get to know her, and even showed an interest in her activities outside of work. Once, she laughed at one of his jokes as she brushed her hair aside, revealing the nape of her neck. She was flirting with him then. Of that, Dwayne is certain.

But where did he go wrong?

With a resounding grunt, he racks the barbell and turns to Sarah. But a man doing deadlifts now occupies the station beside him. While Dwayne had been stewing in anger and embarrassment, Sarah must've slipped away. Leaving his weight station without re-racking or wiping, he heads to the locker room.

Dwayne rinses off and spritzes himself with Christian Dior Sauvage. Its zesty burst does nothing to soothe his irritation, though the spicy pepper kick gives him an idea. Sarah isn't the type of woman who goes for simple drinks. No, Dwayne realizes, she'll need a grander gesture. Something that will show him to be the thoughtful, caring gentleman she needs in her life.

Returning to his cubicle, Dwayne's desire for Sarah usurps any ambition he had to surpass her on the company's leaderboard. With fifteen minutes left before his break ends, he sets to work on research.

Browser tab after browser tab takes Dwayne to

images of expensive flowers and high-class dining, yet none seem quite right for Sarah. She's disciplined, professional, and athletic. On a personal level, her friendliness disarms even the most reclusive coworker while drawing out the best in those around her. Sarah's refined elegance and professionalism inspire even top-tier executives to excellence.

Dwayne closes the tabs in frustration, his mind still on impressing this Sarah Anderson he knows so well. Returning to the day's work, he clicks the call icon on his next contact. On the fifth ring, the call disconnects.

Removing his headset, Dwayne leans back in his chair and rocks. There must be something he can do to catch Sarah's attention. He turns to the woman next to him.

"Say… um…"

"Mr. Church," a uniformed guard says.

Dwayne's eyes, intended to meet his coworker's, stare at the midsection of a burly security guard. His gaze travels upward while heat rises to his neck.

"Yes?"

"Come with me," the officer says.

"What's this about?" Dwayne asks.

The guard walks away. Meanwhile, time seems to slow as he realizes several sets of eyes are on him. He smiles sheepishly at the nameless woman—Carol or Karen—beside him and rises to follow the guard.

Dwayne takes two steps to the guard's one step and catches up with him.

"I asked you a question," Dwayne says.

"I heard you," the guard answers.

Dwayne strains to read the man's lanyard. "Excuse me, but I didn't catch your name."

"I didn't drop it," the guard says and motions toward the manager's office. "Mr. Thompson will see you now."

Upon entering Mr. Thompson's office, Dwayne notices the crack in the right corner of the wall. Then he notices Dali's "Last Supper" framed print above Mr. Thompson's desk. Aside from being off-kilter on the wall, the painting always sets Dwayne on edge, though he could never figure out why. It could be how Christ appears to host his disciples everywhere and nowhere at once.

"Mr. Church?" A woman's voice interrupts Dwayne's musings. "I'm Cynthia Watkins, head of HR. Please have a seat."

Dwayne's eyes linger again on the painting before he complies with Cynthia's request. But when he glances at her, his gaze locks on the fullness of Cynthia's lips and the way they part as if she's about to speak. How has he never noticed her before this moment?

Mr. Thompson clears his throat. "Dwayne. How many years have you worked here?"

A flicker of heat rises to Dwayne's face as he tears his eyes away from the curve of Cynthia's mouth to Mr. Thompson's gaze.

Dwayne responds. "Five years, I think, sir."

"During which," Mr. Thompson says. "Your numbers have been regularly off the charts, beaten only by one other employee."

"Sarah Anderson," Dwayne blurts out, which garners the hardened glares of both Mr. Thompson and Cynthia. "I only know this because my cubicle has a direct line of sight to the leaderboard. That, and Sarah and I chat sometimes at the gym."

Mr. Thompson and Cynthia exchange a cryptic glance, then draw their attention back to Dwayne.

"Mr. Church," Cynthia says. "That's what we wanted to talk with you about." She slides a slip of paper over to Dwayne.

"What's this?" Dwayne asks, scanning the document. It contains names—women's names dating back almost five years. Beside each name is a summary statement. The words "Harassment" and "He can't take no for an answer" slap him in the face.

Damp heat reaches Dwayne's eyes. "I… I don't understand."

"This is our third time having this conversation, Mr. Church," Cynthia says. Her drawn lips and furrowed brow remind him of his mother's disapproving glare. Any attraction he had toward the woman fades away.

"It seems these reports are true. You can't take 'No' for an answer," Mr. Thompson says. "That is why we are terminating your employment with Aspire. Without pressing charges, mind you."

"Please, Mr. Church. Dwayne," Cynthia says. "Learn from your mistakes."

A pink slip slides across the table. In a haze, Dwayne reads it. He wants to protest and confront his accusers, but the voices of Mr. Thompson and Cynthia urge him to sign.

Dwayne scratches out a signature as cockeyed as the painting hovering over Mr. Thompson's head.

"Officer Jackson will escort you to your cubicle to gather your things," Mr. Thompson says. He reaches a hand out to Dwayne. "I'm sorry things had to end in this way. If you need anything—"

"You have thirty days to appeal the termination," Cynthia says as she stands.

Under Officer Jackson's watchful eye, Dwayne returns to his desk and gathers his scant belongings—a coffee mug, his ergonomically designed keyboard, and an award he earned for the highest sales in a month—and tosses them into a file box provided by Aspire Financial Network.

"I'm pretty sure I don't need the box," Dwayne says.

"Suit yourself," Jackson says and turns to leave.

"Wait," Dwayne says.

Jackson turns back toward Dwayne. "Forget something?"

A bead of sweat rolls down Dwayne's back as the officer's eyes bore into him. He left his gym bag in the locker room, but he didn't forget it. No, it's not so much that he forgot, but lost something. The respect of Aspire, for one. And Sarah's friendship.

But why? Did she think he gazed at the firmness of her body too long at the gym? He'd been careful to meet her eyes when he could, so that couldn't be it. Or his approach to her wasn't quite right. Was he too demanding? Did he not listen to what she wanted?

"Mr. Church," the gruff voice of Officer Jackson breaks Dwayne away from the mental spiral of *should-haves* and *if-onlys*.

"Can we go to my locker?"

"Negative," Jackson says. "But HR will have your things sent to you. I'm under strict orders to escort you from the building."

"Right," Dwayne says, following the burly officer through the sales floor.

For Dwayne, the march toward the parking lot feels more like he's being paraded through the building, an allegory for how not to interact with women. However, the incomprehensibility of his termination weighs on his mind.

Upon arrival at his car—a 2025 Ford Explorer—he turns to Officer Jackson.

"Thanks, I guess."

The officer nods and steps away from the vehicle as Dwayne presses start and creeps toward the exit. He turns right on the main road and hits the gas pedal until the speedometer dial rises toward ninety miles an hour.

As the speedometer needle surpasses ninety, thoughts of Sarah Anderson flood his mind—the curve of her lips, the blue of her eyes, her soft laughter, and the way the world seems to brighten in her presence.

Then come the snapshots—a tanned and radiant Sarah smiling against the backdrop of a sun-drenched beach; Sarah, her backpack straining under its weight, framed by the deep green of a forest; and finally, Sarah in New York City, dwarfed by towering skyscrapers and surrounded by a bustling crowd.

As realization hits him, Dwayne slams on the brakes and slaps the steering wheel.

"Dammit!" He shouts and repeats the refrain as cars blow by him, horns honking in annoyance.

Hitting the right turn signal, Dwayne pulls to the side of the road and cuts the engine.

"Drinks and dinner?" Dwayne asks. "How could I have been so stupid? I should've asked her out on a hike or something."

But Dwayne realizes he will not get another chance with Sarah Anderson unless he stages something grand.

But will she listen?

As his gaze falls upon the glove compartment, it occurs to him that Sarah may require a bit of persuasion to relax and have fun.

"Welcome to Buddy Burger," Chris Little says. "Can I

take your order?"

On the other end of the intercom, a woman speaks through static, and a wailing child makes it difficult for Christ to catch every word of the order.

Chris repeats the order back to her. "That's a Number Twelve, no ketchup or lettuce. A Junior Buddy Meal, one large Coke, and one small root beer. Will that be all?"

"That's it," the woman's voice confirms.

Chris grins and tells her to pull up to the next window.

Next to him, his manager, a twenty-something named Todd, claps him on the shoulder. "Not bad for your first official day. You're a natural at this."

"Thanks," Chris beams his infectious smile as the woman with the wailing kid approaches the window.

"That's fourteen, seventy-eight."

The woman hands him a twenty. "Can we have extra napkins? You know, for the kid."

Chris spots the five-year-old sitting in the child-safety seat, a school of cheesy goldfish crackers scattered on the seat beside her.

"Of course," Chris says. He returns with her order, her change, and the extra napkins.

So, it goes like this: car after car, as the after-school crowd bustles past the window. A sedan over-packed with some of his high school friends makes a huge order. When it stops at his window, the football team captain leans out the window and teases Chris, "You're going to make manager soon."

Chris laughs. "I hope so, but it's only my first day."

"Look at you," a cheerleader crammed next to the football captain says. "Making the big bucks."

"Something like that," Chris says, wishing them a good day as they drive off.

With thirty miles between him and Aspire Financial, Dwayne can't help but smile. Though it took some convincing, Sarah Anderson sits in the passenger seat beside him.

"There's still plenty of road between us and the entrance to Look Out Peak; you hungry?"

"Hungry?" Sarah says. "Fuck you, Dwayne. You dragged me against my will into your car, and now you ask if I'm hungry?"

Dwayne can't say her response surprises him. While on the road back to Aspire, it occurred to him that Sarah may have been sending mixed messages or playing hard to get. But it didn't matter now that she had agreed to a date with him.

Beside him, Sarah's hand slips over her stomach, and her fingers press against the smooth fabric of her blouse.

"You're hungry," Dwayne says, glancing at Sarah. She removes her hand and places it on her shaking knee. "You could've asked to stop. There's a Buddy Burger off the next exit. We can order something from the drive-through."

"You think so?" Sarah asks, her voice a whisper and her eyes fixating on a scratch in the console. "And after we eat, you expect us to do what, exactly? I'm not dressed for a hike."

He glances at Sarah, his eyes lingering on her face as if noticing how the sunlight catches in her hair. She removes a hair tie from her purse and pulls her hair back from her face. A few strands escape the grip of the tie. She squints against the setting sun while closing the top of her blouse.

As she turns toward him, he returns his attention to the road. "Sorry about the top button."

Sarah shrugs. "What's with you, anyway, Dwayne?"

"I'm not sure what you mean," Dwayne says.

"I'm sure you don't," Sarah replies, leaning toward the passenger window as the car approaches the exit.

"Don't," Dwayne says, his tone much sharper than he intends.

Sarah recoils away from the door and sinks back into her seat.

"That's better," Dwayne says.

"If you say so," Sarah says, her voice cracking.

Easing the Explorer around the exit ramp, Dwayne smiles to himself. Sarah's nervous—that much he understands—but who wouldn't be nervous on a first date? They just need time to settle in, and sharing a meal would help.

"Now," Dwayne says as he pulls up to the drive-through. "I'm just going to order for the both of us, okay?"

Sarah chews on her bottom lip and nods.

"Excellent," Dwayne says.

The car before him pulls forward, and Dwayne comes face-to-face with the intercom. While he waits for the server on the other end to speak, he scans the menu, then glances with a smile at Sarah.

Chris offers his usual greeting through the intercom and waits. With no response, he tries again.

"Welcome to Buddy—"

"Uh... yeah..." a man's voice crackles through the intercom. "I'll have the number two, and... what'll you have?"

Chris hears a woman's voice mumble something.

"What's that?" the man asks.

"Sir, are you...?" Chris begins.

The woman's voice shouts an expletive, followed by the man's hushed tones.

"Sir, you'll have to speak into the intercom," Chris says.

Chris realizes someone else has joined him at his station and turns.

"Everything okay?" Todd asks.

"I'm not sure," Chris says.

"You still there?" the man's voice asks. "She'll have a salad and a Diet Coke."

Chris repeats the entire order to him, adding, "That'll be seventeen ninety-eight. Please pull up to the next window."

As Chris takes the next order, a Ford Explorer approaches his window. Upon finishing the order, he leans out the window and smiles at the man as he receives a twenty. Beyond the intensity of the man's eyes, he catches the woman's glance. With pleading eyes, she mouths the words, "Help me." Chris grimaces and returns to the register.

Counting out the change with deliberation, Chris processes the woman's appearance—the smeared makeup, the welt on her face, the disheveled hair and rumpled business suit, the way she shrunk away from the man, her body tense.

Creating distance between himself and the drive-through window, Chris signals for Todd.

"What's up, Chris?" Todd asks.

Chris hushes his manager. "The woman's in danger."

Outside, the man shouts and honks the horn.

Todd nods. "Should I handle it?"

"No," Chris says. "Call the police. Tell them it's a domestic issue."

"Right," Todd says. "So, I should handle it while you —"

"No," Chris says. "That'll make him suspicious. I'll stall them. Where's the guy's order?"

Outside, the horn honks again. "Hey, buddy!" the man shouts, then follows it up with a laugh.

"What a prick," Todd grunts. "Chris, be careful."

Squaring his shoulders, Chris turns back to the window. From this distance, he sees the woman clawing at the man, while he attempts to push her away or pull her closer.

Chris hesitates, his eyes dart—register, ice-bucket—there. The drinks. He snatches them up and bolts toward the window.

The woman's eyes widen. "He's got a—"

"Sir, here's your—"

Chris launches the soda into the car window, and the man's face twists in rage.

"I'm terribly sorry," Chris says, backing away. "Let me get—"

A muzzle flashes as a shot rings out. Pain sears through Chris's shoulder and he collapses onto the floor.

Todd and another coworker appear beside Chris, applying pressure to his wound.

Through the haze, Chris hears the slamming of a car door and the rapid clicking of retreating footsteps.

Sirens blare in the distance as Todd continues to apply pressure. "You did good, Chris. Just hold on!"

Chris awakens to the steady beeping of machinery and the glow of hospital lights—his shoulder throbs where the bullet had torn through him. Thanks to Todd's quick actions, he was alive.

The door opens, and his mother enters.

"Baby," she says with a smile, though her puffy, red eyes give away her anguish.

"How long have I been out?" Chris asks.

"Five hours," his mother says, sitting beside him and taking his hand. "There's someone here to see you."

Chris follows his mother's gaze toward the door, where a nurse pushes a young woman in a wheelchair.

"Chris," his mother says. "I'd like you to meet the woman you saved. This is Sarah Anderson."

Chris winces with pain as he struggles to sit up. "I did what anyone would have done."

Sarah shakes her head. "Not anyone. You spilled those drinks, giving me the distraction I needed to escape."

"But the bruising on your face and arms?" Chris asks.

"When he forced me into his car," Sarah says. "That man. Dwayne Church. Even now, his name is bitter in my mouth. I thought I made myself clear, but he kept persisting. It wasn't until HR…"

Her voice trails off into tears.

"Hey," Chris says. "You're safe now."

Sarah sniffs and steadies her voice. "Thanks to your quick thinking, Dwayne's in custody now. I owe you my life, and I don't take that lightly."

Chris flashes her a smile. "Maybe you can repay me by putting in a good word to my manager."

"I will," Sarah says. "And when you're older, I can hook you up with an internship. Though, probably not at Aspire."

There Was an Old Woman Who Thought She Was Dead

• • ● • •

Donna Doty

Magical Realism

"I must be dead," she said aloud, "and if only I can find my body that'll prove it." So, the old woman began searching her tiny cottage beginning with the most likely place, which was her bed, knowing most elderly expire there and finding nothing out of the ordinary looked next in her favorite chair, and again finding nothing moved onto the bathtub, which is a site of particular peril for the aged; but this too yielded naught. With increasing urgency, the old woman extended her search to places of less risk and likelihood until eventually she ended up rummaging the entire house from top to bottom.

The hunt uncovered no body, however, not even the remains of one; but she was not discouraged. Perhaps I was about my gardening and died of a heart attack or heat stroke, she thought; it's been known to happen to old people before and went outback to inspect her cherished rose garden. As earlier, no body was found. "This is peculiar, very peculiar indeed," she declared to the melancholy roses drooping on the bush, "for I am sure I am dead. I expect you are aware of this, my darlings, or you would not languish so. Have I not cared for you as my own children? And so you are, and still, you wither like forsaken orphans. No doubt it is for want of attention you perish," she surmised crossly, "shame on the new owners for not minding you. Shall I give you a little water then, while I still can?" And the old woman watered her beloved roses for the third time that day.

It stands to reason my body was taken away, she reckoned, and yet I have no recollection of it. I expect the new owners had it removed. The odor must have been something awful by then. It was right they got rid of it. "I once heard a ghost story," she explained to her roses as she watered them, "in which the sole occupant of a house died without knowing it. New owners soon took up residency unbeknownst to the original inhabitant and ordered things quite differently, as newcomers are wont to do. The furniture was conspicuously rearranged and some of the owner's belongings were moved about or discarded altogether. Naturally the previous occupant couldn't fathom how she misplaced possessions, nor why letters no longer came, and visitors no longer called. Which incidentally explains how several of my effects have been mislaid of late. Just this morning my spectacles went missing only to turn up unexpectedly on the kitchen table, and you know I always set them on the nightstand before turning in. I shall have to have a word with the new owners about this."

After watering her roses, the old woman decided to venture into town to see if someone would take notice of her. "I may not be able to find my body," she mused, "but a spirit cannot be seen, and I shall know conclusively whether or not I am dead should anyone observe me." It was some distance to the neighboring village and the old woman was loath to make the journey for she was not as spry as she used to be, and walking was unkind to her rheumatism.

She lived at the farthest most end of town in a broken-down specter of a house, if you could still call it a house; that might seem uninhabited to a passerby, if there was a passerby, but no one passed by. The last time anyone stopped by was to deliver the post, and that was many years before. The old woman received no correspondence these days, and as for visitors, it's been some time since she welcomed her last guest. Nevertheless, she resigned herself to the journey, saying, "Oh well, I suppose it is necessary, and if I must walk to town, I must."

Almost at once she remembered she was dead and just as immediately replaced resignation with self-reproach. "Whatever is the matter with me," she scolded, "a spirit has no need of walking; I shall simply glide into town." And with this glorious idea dancing in her head, eagerly readied herself for the outing. The old woman reserved a special dress for those occasional trips to the village, and although the visits had become fewer over the years, it remained in the cupboard yet, waiting fresh and newly pressed.

She felt unusually giddy as she clothed and did seemingly glide without effort about the room to a favorite tune playing on the Victrola. I shall wear just a hint of lipstick today, as well, she thought; and why not, a person should look her best, spirit or no. But I will not be like those old ladies who over-apply on account of their cataracts; oh no, that will never do; I must take care or look a fright. In the looking glass, a much younger woman gazed back at her with perfectly appliquéd lips. She decided to forgo her cane in favor of gliding.

The lane that passed in front of her cottage had not altered much over the years, and as the old woman trudged along, she took note of the many signposts that recalled her journey down the road before. Each and every aspect was both familiar and new and she delighted in the newness and took comfort in old acquaintances. The houses, the flowers, the fences, the trees: some changed, some remained the same. I hope it shan't be much longer now, she thought to herself, a little anxiously. And some time later happily exclaimed: "There! Is that not my old friend, the Lilac tree, at the end of the field? It used to mark the halfway place for me." Upon reaching it, she decided to rest a little while on a dilapidated split-rail fence that previously enclosed a cow pasture. The tree had almost entirely overrun the fence, but there was one small space free of shrubbery where it went lacking and just the right size for her diminutive frame to set upon, so she did and leaned against a post for support.

The walk was more taxing than anticipated and she rather wished she had not left her cane behind. The dead do not come by their ghost legs easily, she realized and longed for her promised glide. Soon she succumbed to the hypnotic cadence of buzzing insects, soothing fragrances and gentle breezes, and dozed off awhile. As she slumbered, she dreamt she drifted high above the trees.

The old woman awoke just in time to glimpse a passerby hiking on a well-traveled thoroughfare that intersected her tiny lane some meters afield. The lone backpacker was moving in her direction and fairly swiftly but had only just crossed the lane, so she attempted a greeting. Her 'hello" had barely left her lips, however, before the traveler managed to put distance between them, quickly becoming a speck in the road. As the speck disappeared completely, she wondered whether she had been observed sitting there. It did not appear so. The haste, the detachment, the lack of acknowledgment all suggested she was not noticed at all. But the true test was yet to come. I shan't make my final decision until I have gathered more evidence, she determined wisely and started once more for the village.

The second half of her journey proved more difficult than the first. For one thing, she turned onto the main road, which was populated by dales and knolls; and for another, previous rainfall caused little mud-filled furrows to form and stones to unearth where rainwater streamed the hummocks and washed away topsoil—all making it hazardous for a frail woman to traverse. Beyond these, the many irregularities inflamed her rheumatism.

It took all her concentration to keep upright, and she dared not take her eyes from the road. She walked ever so slowly and stole only tiny peeks toward her destination when her bearing absolutely required it. At this rate, she thought, it will be noonday before I arrive, but I suspect I'll arrive all the same. When walking became intolerable, she paused to rest and gauge how much farther she had to go. "If memory serves me, it shouldn't be much beyond that large knoll, but I will know for sure once I've mounted it." With great effort she began the ascent and as she did, an opinion took form: it wasn't easy being dead; there appeared no advantages whatsoever for what ailed the body. "Here it is, my phantom rheumatism has come back to haunt me," she sighed, "and I did so hope to leave it behind."

With body bent low and eyes fastened on the road, the old woman eventually reached the top of the rise, and as she peaked its crest, she thought, at last I shall know the distance to town. But she never had the chance to study this. Unhappily her arrival coincided with that of a racing bike moving at great speed up the opposite side of the hill, and at that precise moment she was carelessly sideswiped. The cyclist gave no warning signal as is customary upon encountering a blind spot, and the near collision with an unforeseen obstacle unbalanced the old woman and sent her toppling into a gully.

She let out a little cry as she fell; then managed a more forceful shout for help, but the rider neither stopped nor offered apology and by that time was already half-a-kilometer away. As she lay where she tumbled and wondered what to do, she thought it curious no noise emitted from the cyclist, as is often involuntary with accidental occurrences as these; but not a gasp, not a cuss, not a distress cry of any kind was raised. It was as though I was not seen at all, she realized. "Yes," she said, "I am quite certain I am dead."

The old woman had landed in a tender patch of mud that suffused the gully, and seeing as though she was worn out and having no desire just yet to move from her soft bed, decided to rest there awhile and ponder her lack of existence. As she closed her eyes, a strange sound became apparent, faint at first then fervent. It was a whirring noise, like that of a thousand insects rubbing their legs together or flailing their wings. Soon the drone became palpable, and she felt a rush of cool air amid a spray of moisture and soil as the swarm descended upon the tract of road that ran aside the ditch.

Weary as she was, she determined to know the source, really more out of curiosity than fear, and struggled to open her eyes. Her vantage point from the ground offered little illumination, however. Greeting her was a flurry of moving color, and several moments elapsed before her eyes acclimated themselves to the vision: a herd of bicycles traveling at an alarming rate. The cyclists themselves made no sound and appeared as a single organism in thought and movement as they raced down the hill and beyond. Were she able, the old woman needed to extend her hand but a little to touch them, except the human horde, intent upon the prize, took no notice of her lying there, mere millimeters from where machine met earth. "It's true then, I'm not here," she acknowledged, without a hint of loss or regret.

Still, there was an instant when she thought she made

eye contact with one of the cyclists and caught a glimmer of recognition; yet the enormous pace by which they passed soon rendered this notion equally fleeting and she had to concede she imagined it. At no point during the mad migration did the woman consider shouting for help; it simply did not occur to her. Her eyes slowly closed, and she contemplated the horde's chances of overtaking the lead cyclist, who by now must have surely put kilometers between them, and silently cheered on the solitary racer who was the cause of her present predicament. The mishap had unwittingly connected them, and her final thoughts were only of winning.

The following morning a swarm of flies refused to pass her by and brought her body to the attention of the local dustmen. *What is it? Looks like a crone just up and died here. Better remove the body then before the stench becomes something awful.* And not knowing what else to do, they placed her body on the cart with the day's trash.

About the Authors

ROBERT PLANT

Robert Plant self-published his debut novel, Heartstrings, in 2023 and has a knack for stirring the soul in his fiction writing. After releasing this family drama to the world, Robert pivoted to writing in the Sci-Fi genre. He's finalizing his next book, Dark Matter, to be released in the summer of 2025, which will be an anthology of short stories that will challenge our existence in this small sliver of the cosmos. These short stories are created with a likeness to The Twilight Zone and Black Mirror shows and will have you on the edge of your seat until the final twist.

SCOTT MEEHAN

Scott A. Meehan is a retired Army veteran, middle school history teacher, and award-winning author. He is a Bronze Star recipient from actions in Iraq and is known for his storytelling based on his worldwide experiences as a missionary kid and Army veteran. Meehan writes multi-cultural themes that focus on current events in the form of thrillers, suspense, romance, and military. He has a BA in Secondary Education-Social Sciences, MA in Computer Resource Information Management, and an MBA. In 2024, Scott won first place in the Orlando

Veteran's Creative Arts Awards contest with his creative short story, *CH-47A Chinooks: Guardians of the Sky*.

DONALD FIRESMITH

Donald Firesmith is a multi-award-winning author of speculative fiction, including science fiction, fantasy, paranormal horror, and modern urban paranormal novels and collections of short stories. Because of his strong background in software/system engineering and science, his science fiction is well-researched, and he relies on numerous science, technology, and military technical advisors to ensure that the non-speculative aspects of his stories are realistic and believable.

MICHAEL NELSON

Michael Nelson is a former small-town physician, living in a small community among the deep hills and valleys of Southwestern Wisconsin. Retired now, he indulges in his many hobbies. Woodworking, and travel to various parts of the country but most of all; writing. Always being open to new things has kept him youthful and vital as he tries to keep up with his young daughter, Isabelle Drawing upon their adventures together, in this most recent endeavor, he and his daughter, Isabelle have taken a lighter approach to exciting adventure and magic.

D. KRAUSS

D. Krauss resides in the Shenandoah Valley, Virginia. He has been a cottonpicker, a sodbuster, a librarian, a surgical orderly, the guy who paints the little white line down the middle of the road, a weatherman, a door-kickin' shove-gun-in-face lawman, a hunter of terrorists, and a school bus driver. Currently, he's a layabout. He's been married over 45 years (yep, same woman), and has a wildman bass guitarist for a son.

ED DEJESUS

Ed DeJesus (pronounced D Geezus) joined Indies United in January 2025. His thriller novel, *The Vulnerable,* debuted in April. His short story offers a glimpse into his forthcoming memoir collection, *Simpler Times in The Spindle City.* A technopreneur, he was President of Sightline Solar, CEO of JustZip.com, and VP of Engineering for MSL. Previously, his software work at Digital Equipment Corp was published in the Artificial Intelligence (AI) and Design Automation journals. He served in the US Army Reserves and opened a record store with his wife in the vinyl era. He resides in Florida and is a Gulf Coast Writers Association member. When Ed's not immersed in his writing, he finds joy in reading, dancing, singing Karaoke, and traveling the world with his wife and children.

LISA TOWLES

Lisa Towles is an award-winning crime novelist and a passionate speaker on the topics of fiction writing, creativity, and self care. She has thirteen crime thrillers in print with a new thriller, Switch, due for release in 2025. Her E&A Series titles Hot House and Salt Island were both Amazon Kindle #1 Bestsellers. Lisa is a member of Mystery Writers of America, Sisters in Crime, and International Thriller Writers. Deeply committed to supporting other writers, she hosts a YouTube series called Story Impact, where she interviews authors about the meaning and impact of their books. Lisa has an MBA in IT Management and works full-time in the tech industry in the San Francisco Bay area.

TIMOTHY BALDWIN

Timothy Baldwin grew up in Syracuse, New York. He currently resides in Maryland where he teaches English, Creative Writing, Film, and Theatre on the middle school level. At the insistence of his own students, he began writing seriously in 2014. He credits his love for story to his mother, who spent countless hours reading to him and his siblings when they were growing up. Growing up, he devoured the literary words of C. S. Lewis, J. R. R. Tolkien, Piers Anthony, and many others. Mysteries, thrillers, and fantasies are among the genre he most frequently reads. When he's not writing, he's reading, teaching, camping, or enjoying a live music concert.

DONNA DOTY

Donna L. Doty, Ph.D. is a New York-based Sociologist, content creator, and 2D animator who writes and produces her own animations series, *Coffee with Katrin*. Most recently, Donna wrote a work of speculative fiction called *The Rule of Thoughts: A Fictional Treatise in the*

Sociology of Knowledge—which received a Certificate of Appreciation from the International Fiction Festival in 2024 for being ranked in the top 10% in the Novel category among 850 authors from 48 countries. Donna also wrote several short stories including *There Was an Old Woman Who Thought She Was Dead*, *The Day We Saw a Giraffe in Our Yard,* and *The Red Spot*. She is currently working on a short story series.

Thank you for taking the time to read this collection from Indies United Publishing House. We hope you enjoyed it and would like to encourage you to take a moment to review this collection on your favorite reading platform.

A little about Indies United

Here at Indies United, we are a co-op of like-minded authors working together to showcase our books and highlight our diversity as writers. We openly encourage and support both new and established authors in their pursuit of finding their audience while bringing to you books worth reading. Our goal is to give authors a home to call their own, while bringing fresh, innovative, and exciting books to readers all over the world.

If you are an author, please check us out at www.indiesunited.net

www.ingramcontent.com/pod-product-compliance
Lightning Source LLC
Chambersburg PA
CBHW071528120726
47907CB00013B/1254